"What was I supposed to do?"

Gracie asked the question calmly. "Have Miss Jackson declared a health risk and tossed out of the building?"

"I can do without your sarcasm," Morgan said softly. "You could have told her I wasn't in.... I don't like women coming into my office. It's a part of my life which has nothing to do with them. If Alex shows up again, perhaps you could make that clear."

Gracie nodded slowly, anger bubbling inside her like a tiny volcano waiting to explode.

"I gather you don't approve?"

She looked at him coolly. "It's not a question of whether I approve or disapprove, Mr. Drake. I don't think it's my place to provide alibis for you when you've become bored with your latest possession and you no longer want her around...."

CATHY WILLIAMS

a powerful attraction

Harlequin Books

TORONTO • NEW YORK • LONDON
AMSTERDAM • PARIS • SYDNEY • HAMBURG
STOCKHOLM • ATHENS • TOKYO • MILAN

Harlequin Presents first edition November 1991
ISBN 0-373-11413-3

Original hardcover edition published in 1990
by Mills & Boon Limited

A POWERFUL ATTRACTION

CHAPTER ONE

Now that she was finally outside the airport, Gracie was surprised to find that it was much hotter than she had expected. Before she had left England, she had cursorily scanned the succinct temperature guide in the newspaper to see what she could expect when she arrived in New York, but her mind had been too full of things to really pay much attention.

How was she to know, when she'd left behind a cool, drizzly English summer day, that she would land in soaring sunshine and temperatures in the eighties?

She stripped off her jacket, shoved up the sleeves of the thin blue and white striped cotton shirt, and plunged into the nearest yellow taxi she could see, instantly breathing a sigh of relief that it was air-conditioned. She gave the cab driver the name of the hotel where she was staying, and settled back against the seat with her eyes closed. She might just as well savour what would probably prove to be the last bit of relative relaxation for the next couple of weeks!

A gut feeling told her that she had said goodbye to any real hope of peace and quiet when she had received Jenny's letter four days ago. It had been brief, but then Jenny's letters always were. Brief, intermittent, and somehow leaving the impression that they had been hurriedly scribbled either just at the end of an exhausting day out doing something exciting, or else in the rushed fifteen minutes spent waiting to be picked up for an exhausting day out doing something exciting.

Jenny was in trouble. Gracie had read the large, childish handwriting with a sinking feeling. Only seven months in New York, and already she was in trouble.

5

More than that, she expected Gracie to fly halfway across the world, using up almost all her savings, to bail her out.

Hadn't that always been the case? Jenny landing herself in scrapes which most sensible people managed to easily avoid, and then assuming that her faithful, dependable sister would be only too happy to sail to the rescue?

Gracie glared in frustration at the five-storey hotel in front of which the taxi had drawn up, and only just managed to squeeze out a smile when the taxi driver said to her, 'It's cheap, lady, but it's not *that* bad!'

She was tempted to reply that the quality of the hotel was the very least of her problems. Instead she threw him a watery grin and lugged her suitcase up to the small reception desk, where the thick-set middle-aged receptionist handed her the bedroom key, informed her that there was no porter, and advised her to avoid the lifts.

She hadn't expected a great deal from the hotel, considering that it was just about the cheapest she could find in downtown Manhattan, and she wasn't pleasantly surprised. The bedroom was small, with the regulation portable television, two over-large prints of forest scenes, and just about enough cupboard space to hold the clothes which she had brought over to last the fortnight.

There was also a telephone. Gracie looked at it, and decided to have a bath before she used it to call her sister. Besides, she needed to think. Life, she thought wryly. Just when you thought you had jumped a hurdle, you looked ahead only to find that there were ten more staring you in the face.

Seven months ago, she had seen Jenny off from Heathrow Airport with a feeling of relief. Much as she loved her sister, things were so much easier when she was not around.

Jenny had landed herself a plum job in New York, working for Morgan Drake, *the* Morgan Drake, as one of his four private secretaries, and Gracie had waved goodbye to her wild, reckless younger sister with the hope that the experience of living abroad would mature her.

'My troublemaking days are over!' Jenny had promised, crowing at her luck. 'I'll be in a position of responsibility, and I intend to be as good as gold. When you next see me, you won't recognise me.'

'I live in hope, Jen,' Gracie had replied truthfully. 'I'm going prematurely grey at having to keep my eye on you twenty-four hours a day.'

Their parents had died in a road accident when Gracie was eighteen. Jenny was then only just thirteen, and already a handful. As she grew out of her lanky, girlish adolescence to emerge a beautiful, curvaceous blonde, Gracie had bade a reluctant farewell to her own youth, had found a job as a secretary to one of the local lawyers, and braced herself for the never-ending task of trying to keep her sister in check.

Why, oh, why, she now thought with frustrated resignation, had Jenny managed to ruin everything by getting herself into yet another scrape? Surely working for someone like Morgan Drake would have been enough to shake a little sense into that head of hers? Gracie had never personally met him, but she read the newspapers, and had enough rudimentary knowledge about the business world to know that he was not a man to be tampered with. Why on earth had that legendary ruthlessness not been enough to inject some long-delayed sobriety into her sister?

Her stomach was rumbling from lack of food. Gracie ignored it and instead slipped on the only sleeveless dress she had brought, a flowered affair which she had admitted in the past did nothing for her but which she had hung on to anyway.

She had planned on calling Jenny, but decided to go to the hospital directly instead. She knew her sister, a talented amateur actress if ever. Gracie had no intention of allowing her an hour to prepare her facial expressions in order to elicit the maximum amount of sympathy. Oh, no.

She caught another cab, this time to the New York Hospital on Seventh Avenue, and decided that she had better make it her last or else run the risk of exhausting her limited supply of spending money before the two weeks were up.

Jenny was lying in bed when Gracie walked in, one leg bandaged and suspended from a pulley attached to the ceiling. There were elasticated bandages around her left wrist, and more just visible under the thin pink material of her nightie. Her blonde hair fanned out around her face and, although she looked drawn, she was certainly not in the agony of pain that she had suggested in her letter.

When she looked up and saw Gracie, her pink mouth half opened in surprise.

'Gracie!' she yelped excitedly. 'You're here! I was expecting you tonight! Or tomorrow morning! I would have met you at the airport, but...' She gestured at her leg and smiled ruefully.

'I managed to change my flight to an earlier one.' Gracie walked across to the bed and kissed her sister on the cheek. 'You don't look as bad as I was expecting,' she said drily. 'You said in your letter that you were broken everywhere and that you'd be lucky to ever get back on your feet again. I've been worried sick about you!'

'Three broken ribs, a broken leg and a sprained wrist.' Jenny rattled off her injuries with the faintest trace of pride in her voice.

'How did it happen?'

'Car accident,' she replied succinctly.

'I know that much,' Gracie persevered patiently, 'but your letter wasn't exactly overflowing with details. All it said was that you were in hospital and needed me to come over desperately.' She sighed and looked at the flushed face with its halo of golden curls. Angelic. Shame

the impression was skin-deep only. She was relieved that
Jenny's condition was not serious, but it was beginning
to dawn on her that perhaps she had been dragged all
the way from London on what might well prove to be
an unnecessary trip. 'Was anyone else hurt?'

'Oh, no.' Jenny lifted one slim shoulder in a shrug
and lowered her wide blue eyes. Gracie almost clicked
her tongue with impatience. She was hiding something.
She had spent too long looking after her sister not to
recognise when the truth was being conveniently
abridged.

'Care to elaborate?' she asked with fortitude.

'Well . . . there *was* someone else in the car, but he got
off with cuts and bruises.'

'Who was he?' Gracie prepared herself for the worst.
From as far back as she could remember, Jenny had gone
out with the most unsuitable men and had laughed off
her sister's objections with a careless nonchalance.

'Morgan Drake's nephew.'

'Your boss's nephew?'

'Do you have to say it in that tone of voice?' Jenny
looked up with a trace of defiant sullenness.

Gracie contemplated the childlike, downturned mouth
and suddenly thought how much nicer it would have been
to be back in England, in her flat, in her bed and with
no prospects whatsoever of having to contend with her
headache of a sister. At least not for the time being.

'What were you doing with Morgan Drake's nephew?'
she asked, feeling as though she were trying to get blood
from a stone. 'And why do I get the feeling that he's
somehow tied up with my being over here? You never
mentioned him in any of your letters.'

'We've been seeing each other for a while now.'

There was a short silence, while Gracie digested this
information, then she said crisply, 'Well, I'm glad he
wasn't hurt. Isn't that always the way? The driver escapes
unscathed and the passenger bears the brunt of the injuries. Though you could have explained all this to me

in your letter—why insist that I come all the way over here when you can quite happily recover on your own? You even have a room to yourself, and that's saying something.' She glanced around the room for the first time, taking in the colour television with video recorder, the matching and very un-hospital-like linen, the attractive wicker dressing-table.

'Rickie insisted that Morgan pay for me to have a room on my own, or else I would have been in shared facilities.'

Again that sheepish look came into Jenny's eyes, and again Gracie had the uneasy feeling that the full story was far from told.

'Generous man, your boss,' Gracie commented neutrally, trying to figure out what was going on in her sister's head. Whatever was being hidden would eventually emerge, but from experience she knew that it was no good at all trying to force it out. Jenny had always backed away from pressure, even pressure of the well-meaning variety. Far better to wait for the truth to unravel itself.

'Morgan's not too thrilled with me at the moment,' Jenny finally commented, with the reluctance of someone forced into a very unwilling admission.

'Why not? I know you'll be off work for a while, but that's hardly your fault.'

Jenny averted her eyes and plucked nervously at the quilted spread covering her.

'Oh, for heaven's sake, Jen, out with it,' Gracie said impatiently, thoroughly fed up with the cat-and-mouse conversation they seemed to be conducting. 'I'm tired and in no mood to sit here indefinitely playing games.' It was at times like this that her sister made her feel a hundred.

'Gracie, I'm in trouble.'

Oh, lord, Gracie thought with a shudder, I knew there had to be more to it than a broken leg, three broken ribs and a sprained wrist. She had suspected that Jenny would not have asked her to fly to New York just so that she could have some sisterly compassion. She would complain in all her letters from here to doomsday that she was suffering terribly, but in the end she would have been perfectly happy to recover in her own time, with no big sister around to preach at her.

'What kind of trouble?' she asked cautiously.

'Big trouble. Morgan's furious. He may even take legal action against me, Gracie. I was driving the car when it crashed, and it wasn't insured for me.'

'I see.'

They stared at each other, then a tear plopped out of the corner of Jenny's eye and trailed mournfully down her cheek. 'I don't want to leave New York. He could sack me, sue me, make it impossible for me to find work anywhere else. I can't leave, Gracie, I just can't; I'm in love with Rickie!' There was a hint of desperation in her voice.

Gracie looked at her sister, aghast. She had an insane desire to yell at her that she should have borne all those things in mind before she decided to go for a joy-ride behind the wheel of someone else's car, in a foreign country, and with precious little driving experience.

'Has he mentioned any of those possibilities?' Gracie asked after a while.

'Not exactly.'

'What does that mean, for heaven's sake?'

'He hasn't exactly said that he'll take court action, but I just know he will! He doesn't like me. Well, actually he doesn't approve of my seeing his nephew.'

Gracie had the dizzy sensation of being drawn into a whirlpool, and she wearily rubbed her eyes. She felt physically and emotionally drained, and Jenny's desperate pleading wasn't helping matters.

'Why not?'

'He has some old-fashioned idea that Rickie ought to be getting his head down and learning the ropes of the business, and it's all very awkward because he controls the purse-strings.'

'I'm surprised that you haven't called it quits and moved on to fresher pastures,' Gracie said with a hint of sarcasm. She had never known her sister to pursue a man, any man. They had always pursued her. Hadn't that been part of the problem? The house had constantly echoed with the steady hum of eager boyfriends and all the attendant problems.

'Maybe he has a point,' Gracie remarked calmly.

'Don't start taking his side!'

'I'm not taking sides. Don't be ridiculous.'

'The fact is—well, I'm pretty keen on Rickie.' Jenny glanced down at the pale blue sheet, refusing to meet her sister's curious glance. 'I'm scared, Gracie. Scared of what might happen to me if Morgan decides to press charges, and scared of losing Rickie.'

Gracie looked thoughtfully at her sister. There was an air of genuine vulnerability about her that she had never seen before.

'Where do I fit into this scenario?'

'I want you to talk to Morgan.' Before Gracie could voice any protest, Jenny continued hurriedly, 'Try and smooth things over...' Her voice trailed off.

'It's not my place to interfere in your personal life. I can't magically fix it so that Morgan Drake changes his mind about you and his nephew. That's something you'll have to work out between yourselves.'

'I know that. But...well, you could try and persuade him not to take any action against me over the driving incident. He might listen to you. You know how easily I panic, and, well, you're so cool-headed and rational...'

Gracie stifled a grimace. She wondered how it was that what should be virtues somehow managed to sound like boring flaws in her character. But her sister had a point. Where Jenny had always been rash and spontaneous, Gracie had been level-headed and logical. Whether from necessity or not, she could not say. Had she always been like that? Perhaps not. Perhaps she had cultivated it in order to cope with Jenny's charming, irritating, unchangeable waywardness.

Of course she would go and see Morgan, albeit very reluctantly. What choice did she have? Besides, she didn't want a depressed Jenny landing on her doorstep in two months' time any more than Jenny wanted it herself. Coping with a depressed Jenny was worse than coping with the plague.

She remained for a while longer, listening to Jenny and thinking about what she could say to Morgan Drake to persuade him that the unfortunate episode should be chalked down to heady youth. Even she would have found that difficult to buy, and she had no doubt that Morgan Drake, man of the world that he was, would be even more sceptical.

By the time she left the hospital, she was feeling ten years older and thoroughly ill-tempered.

The sun was still spilling down from the sky, blindingly bright against the huge, glassy faces of the skyscrapers. Gracie let her feet carry her along Broadway. Everyone around her appeared to be in a tremendous rush, and there was a constant whine of police cars and fire engines which made the place feel as though it had been lifted from a stage set somewhere.

In different circumstances, it would have been great to wander along, perhaps stopping off for a coffee at one of the hundreds of coffee bars that littered the sides of the streets. Gracie had only been abroad twice in her life, and never before to America. She had originally hoped to take in as many of the tourist sights as she could before she left New York, but right now that was the last thing on her mind.

She pulled out the address of the office block where Morgan Drake worked and looked at it thoughtfully.

This does it, she thought. This was going to be positively the last time that she bailed her sister out of trouble, whatever the reason. Jenny had always been the baby, but it was about time she grew up. Heaven knows,

I've had to grow up quickly enough, she mused without bitterness.

She looked in front of her at the magnificent glass building that rose up into the sky and then down at the sheet of paper in her hand, where she had hurriedly scribbled the address of Drake Industries.

The black and gold sign outside the building said 'Drake Plaza'. Gracie expelled her breath slowly, watching the stream of people entering and leaving the building. She had known that Morgan Drake was rich, Jenny had told her so in her letters, but she had never mentioned that one entire, huge and frighteningly impressive building belonged solely to him.

I don't want to be here, she thought helplessly.

She gritted her teeth together and strode purposefully towards the entrance. Now that she was here, unintentional though her arrival might have been, it would be downright stupid not to go right in and confront Morgan Drake. Take the bull by the horns.

The foyer was as spectacular as the outside of the building promised. There were plants everywhere, lending an impersonal beauty to the cold surroundings. Gracie did not linger long enough to ascertain whether they were real or else just very good imitations. She walked up to the reception desk and said in as authoritative a voice as she could muster that she was there to see Mr Drake.

'Which Mr Drake would that be, miss?'

'Mr Morgan Drake.' Did she sound nervous? She sincerely hoped not. An attack of nerves was definitely the last thing she needed to win her case.

'Do you have an appointment?'

'I'm afraid not, but——'

'Then you'll have to make one with one of his secretaries. Mr Drake's a very busy man. His personal assistants take care of all that.'

'What floor are they on? I'll go and see if I can fix up a time to see him. It's very important,' she said in a determined voice, adding when she could see the receptionist's reluctance to allow her on to the director's floor, 'and of a highly personal nature. I could tell you everything, and you could pass it on to his secretary from here, within hearing of everyone walking past, but I don't think Mr Drake would take too kindly to that. In fact, he might be *very angry*.'

She felt quite pleased with herself when she jumped into the lift and waited for it to swing open on to the top floor.

Who would have thought that getting to see one man would have been as involved as this? Did they think that she had had a bomb concealed underneath her sleeveless flowered dress? The idea made her smile, and she stepped into the spacious office where his secretaries sat with a feeling of self-confidence.

A pregnant, dark-haired woman with a frozen expression of ill-humour on her face sat at the nearest large, U-shaped desk. She was busily typing something and frowning in concentration.

She looked up when Gracie walked in.

'Yes?' she demanded.

'I'm here to see Mr Drake.'

'I don't believe he's expecting anyone. Who are you? How did you get up here? The security guards should know better than to send unauthorised personnel up to this floor. Now, if you don't mind——' She stood up to escort Gracie out of the door.

'I don't believe you understood what I was saying to you,' Gracie said coldly, refusing to budge an inch now that she had made it this far. 'I'm here to see Mr Drake and I have no intention of leaving until I have done just that.'

'Name?' his secretary bit out after a pause, then she dialled through to her boss's office.

'He'll see you,' she said resentfully, after she had replaced the receiver, 'for five minutes. No more. If your interview requires more time, then you'll have to make an appointment through me. And,' she added with a thin smile, 'he's fully booked for the next three weeks.'

Gracie snorted in disgust, then walked towards the black adjoining door and knocked sharply, pushing it open when a voice from inside the room told her to enter.

The man behind the desk was waiting for her. He was sitting in his leather swivel chair, his hands clasped behind his head, an expression of cool curiosity on his face.

This was not what she had been expecting. Shouldn't he have been older? She felt hot red colour flood her cheeks as she took in the hard good looks, the careless self-confidence that was associated with power and wealth.

His hair was thick and black, his eyes light grey. Those light grey eyes were shrewdly assessing her, waiting for her to say something, and she felt an unaccustomed jolt of alarm course through her body.

Pull yourself together, she thought, inwardly cringing at the picture she must be presenting—eyes wide, mouth half open, cheeks flushed with colour. This wasn't like her at all. She was normally so self-controlled and cool, especially with men, a capable lady rather than a sexy one.

'I'm Gracie Temple,' she said, resisting the urge to clear her throat and realising immediately that she was stating the obvious. Hadn't his secretary announced her when she had phoned through? 'I've come to talk to you about my sister, Jennifer Temple.'

'Do you make it a habit to stampede your way into people's offices when you have something to say to them?' He spoke in an amused, lazy voice, but he was watching her very carefully. A feeling of acute self-consciousness swept over Gracie. It suddenly struck her that her little cotton dress must appear wildly out of place in these plush surroundings. No wonder his secretary had looked at her with such reptilian disdain. Perhaps, she thought, it wasn't such a hot idea to come here on the spur of the moment after all. Perhaps she should have dressed more carefully for the part. How could she hope to win anyone over in a flowered cotton dress?

When he motioned her to the chair opposite his desk she sat down with a feeling of relief. At least in the safety of the chair she did not feel quite so much like a microbe being coldly scrutinised by a mildly curious scientist. Did this man normally have such an effect on women? She felt that, had they met in different circumstances, he would have perhaps glanced at her for no more than a few seconds, then dismissed her. Gracie felt a swift, inexplicable pang which she hid behind a cool, polite expression.

'So you're Jennifer Temple's sister,' Morgan drawled. There was an undertone of amusement in his voice that Gracie did not care for.

'That's right,' she assented neutrally. 'I've just come from the hospital, and she's very worried. About the accident.'

'So she should be. Did she fill you in on all the gory details?'

'Of course she did!' Gracie snapped, forgetting that she was supposed to be on her best behaviour, that in fact she had come here in the first place to ask a favour from this man. He rattled her. Everything about him unnerved her, made her feel awkward and gauche, a teenager.

He raised one eyebrow but the expression on his face didn't change. 'So you know that the car was not insured for her.'

'Yes.'

'And that the Ferrari was completely written off.'

Ferrari? Jenny had not mentioned the make of the car.

'Yes,' Gracie mumbled, wondering what else her sister had conveniently omitted to mention.

'An expensive mistake, don't you think?' he re-marked softly, correctly interpreting the expression of blankness on her face.

'Yes.' Gracie threw him a steely look. The conversation was clearly affording him some amusement.

Was this typical of the American tycoon? she wondered. Did they eventually become as impersonal as their cities of glass towers? Her own boss in London was just the opposite, a middle-aged, grey-haired man with a wife and three children and a sympathetic manner.

It crossed her mind that she should be capable of dealing with Morgan Drake's intimidating self-assurance with her own brand of coldness, but it was proving difficult. Her mind wanted to, but her senses were too sharply focused on his masculinity. Every time she looked at him she was aware of his lean, aggressive body and that sensuous, intelligent face with its hard, bronzed contours.

'What about the role your nephew played in the accident?' she asked tartly, averting her eyes to the window behind his head.

'Oh, he's been reprimanded, believe me.'

He didn't expand and he didn't need to. The initial impact of that ruthless face had been enough to tell Gracie that Morgan Drake was not a man to look leniently on irresponsible behaviour.

'So your sister's imported you from England to come over here and fight her battles on her behalf...?'

It was such an accurate assessment of the situation that Gracie was lost for words. There was a hard, calculating glitter in his eyes, and she felt as though he could see right through to the very mechanism that made her tick, and was secretly laughing at her expense.

She suddenly wondered whether her five minutes were up. He didn't appear to be making any effort to move, but she would have to speak her piece quickly or else risk having to come back and relive this nightmare all over again. The prospect did not thrill her. Morgan Drake made her feel uncomfortable, there was no denying that. More uncomfortable, in fact, than she had felt in the presence of anyone, for a very long time.

'I'm not an item of luggage, Mr Drake,' she informed him in a precise voice. 'Jenny didn't import me. She needed my help and I came over here to give it. It's called sisterly love.'

'It's called finding someone else to do your dirty work for you.'

'I resent that!' Gracie stood up, her eyes flashing with fury. Just who did he think he was? She was not used to such directness, had never encountered it before.

'Ah!' he intoned with satisfaction, 'I knew that there had to be some fire burning behind that prim English exterior.'

'Why, you——!' Gracie spluttered. Her face was burning and she had to clench her fists to stop herself from leaning across and slapping that smug, speculative smile off his face.

'Oh, sit down,' he said, staring at her flushed face. 'We won't accomplish anything if you let histrionics get in your way.'

A slight smile still played on his lips although his voice was perfectly serious.

Histrionics yourself, Gracie wanted to yell, but instead she sat back down and tried to compose her thoughts.

'Jenny thinks that you might take her to court over the accident,' she said bluntly. 'I'm here to ask you to reconsider, if that's your intention.'

'So you've regained that admirable British self-control . . . you should have been a lawyer, Miss Temple. No wonder your sister imported—sorry, asked you to come over. I can't imagine Jennifer standing up for herself with quite so much articulate fervour . . .'

Gracie thought that he managed to make her cherished composure sound like some sort of affliction. Why hadn't Jenny ever given her a more definite idea of what this man was like? Her letters, the few that there had been, were always so vague, and words like 'cute, but not my type' conveyed nothing at all about the sleek-haired, sleek-limbed man sitting in front of her.

'You're straying from the point, Mr Drake,' she said tightly.

'So I am,' he agreed. He stood up and went across to the wide window and stared down below. Gracie immediately felt at a disadvantage and she wondered whether he was doing it on purpose. She had once read somewhere that a successful ploy to intimidate an adversary was to stand over them, so that they were left feeling inadequate and vulnerable.

'As a matter of fact,' he continued smoothly, 'I never planned on taking any court action against your sister. What I said to her when I went to visit her in the hospital was that she should count her blessings that I wasn't going to pursue the matter to its ultimate conclusion. The silly girl must have misinterpreted the conversation. Her feelings of guilt probably blurred over what I said to her. It was just as well that the accident occurred on the grounds of my estate, or else who knows what line our diligent police force would have taken on the whole thing?'

He allowed the question to hang in the air, filling it with a multitude of unspoken implications.

'I'm grateful,' Gracie said dutifully. If gratitude was what he wanted, then she might as well oblige. Oblige and leave. Immediately. Her face still felt flaming hot and her pulses were tingling with an awareness of him which was embarrassing. Not least because she was all too aware of her physical limitations in the eyes of a man such as this one.

She prepared to rise from her chair. 'Well, that's all I came for, so I won't keep——'

'Not so fast, Miss Temple,' he cut in, swinging around to face her. He placed both his hands firmly on the top of his desk and looked at her. There was something about him. Was it the eyes? Or the aggressive lines of his face?

She couldn't be sure... She looked at the powerfully built body with an unaccustomed trace of confusion. His sleeves had been rolled up to expose tanned, strong arms sprinkled with fine dark hair. Gracie stared at them, wondering inconsequentially where he went to get his tan. California perhaps?

'I want to talk to you about your sister and my nephew. What has she said to you about him?'

Gracie frowned. 'She seems very fond of him,' she hedged, twining her slim fingers together and staring at them. She had a sudden urge to be out of this office, and far away from the disturbing presence of Morgan Drake. She didn't like the effect that he was having on her. He made her feel a bit like a clumsy adolescent, and she was anything but that, for heaven's sake!

'You English are masters of the understatement, aren't you? I find it intriguing.' He let his eyes rest on her for a fraction longer than seemed necessary and Gracie felt her face grow hot. 'Richard seems to think that he's in love with Jennifer. It's a most unsuitable arrangement. You could help me to persuade them both of that.'

'What?' Gracie's head shot up in surprise.

'He's twenty-two, and right now he has a good head on his shoulders. But he needs a lot of hard training here before he can even begin to run this company. The last thing he needs is to be infatuated with an English girl on a one-year secondment to America. Especially one as flighty as your sister.'

'And how exactly do you think I might be of help?' Gracie snapped sarcastically. 'Should I stand guard by the hospital door every day until I return to England? I don't think I would have any influence at all in telling Jenny how to run her personal life. In case you hadn't noticed, she's inclined to be a bit headstrong.' Talk about understatement, Gracie thought laconically. Jenny had never paid the slightest scrap of attention to any of Gracie's remonstrations in the past. She might run to her older sister for help when problems arose, but when it came to men she had always viewed Gracie's attitude with a certain amount of pity.

'You should grab a bit more of life, before it passes you by!' she had once said, and Gracie had interpreted it to mean that she should grab a bit more of men before they passed her by and she was left on the shelf like a can of baked beans that had gone past its expiry date.

'It's something we could work on,' he said non-committally.

'Work on?' Gracie looked at the hard-edged face with astonishment. 'I'm here for exactly thirteen more days. I don't even think that gives me enough time to work on getting round all the tourist sights, far less trying to talk my little sister into giving up your nephew. That would be the sort of uphill task that could take a lifetime to accomplish, and even with that sort of time on my side I wouldn't guarantee success.'

She stood up and bent over for her bag, painfully conscious of his eyes on her.

'You're nothing at all like your sister to look at, are you? I would never in a million years have guessed that you were sisters.'

Gracie stood up and faced him. She could feel the blood rush to her cheeks, but she tilted her chin forward and surveyed him with distaste. She didn't have to ask him what he meant, because she knew exactly what he was getting at. From an early age, Jenny had always been the centre of attention with her striking fair looks and wide blue eyes. The years had been even kinder to her. They had made her legs longer and slimmer, her breasts fuller and more rounded, and her figure even more shapely.

Gracie had become accustomed to living in the shadow of all that beauty. She could understand what Morgan Drake had meant when he told her that she was nothing like her sister to look at. She just wondered what had taken him so long to point it out. He didn't seem to waste much time beating about the bush when it came to anything else.

He was only stating a fact, but it still hurt. Gracie felt her lips tighten.

'No need to look so taken aback.' A slight smile played on his lips, making her feel even more helplessly furious.

'Is your directness a typical American trait,' she enquired curtly, 'or is it just your way?'

'A bit of both, I suspect.'

She was still standing and she felt his eyes sweep over her, taking in her slenderness, her small, high breasts and chestnut hair that fell in a bob straight down to her shoulders. Her eyes were wide and green in colour. They were, Gracie thought, her best feature. On her own, she probably looked all right. It was just that she had had the misfortune to be born with a sister who would make most women look insignificant.

She turned away and walked rapidly to the door. Her hand was on the door-handle when the deep voice said behind her, 'There's something else.'

Gracie looked round, wondering what something else there could possibly be. Hadn't they covered everything? He had had no intention of suing Jenny, and he had implied that she would find no difficulty in staying in New York if she wanted to, despite his opposition to her affair with his nephew.

Now that she had met him, Gracie was as certain as she ever would be of anything that, ruthless or not, Morgan was fair. He might try and talk his nephew out of seeing so much of Jenny, but she was convinced that that was as far as it would go.

So what else could he possibly have to say?

She looked at him questioningly, and she waited for him to continue.

'There's the small matter of your sister's replacement.'

Gracie nodded, a shadow of puzzlement crossing her fine features. What on earth did that have to do with her?

'I specifically wanted someone English so that I could train them in my methods for a year and then transfer them to the offices which are due to open in Europe next fall.'

'Jenny will only be in hospital for about eight weeks or so.'

'Someone will have to cover for her, and I was also considering taking on some additional staff. One of my key personal secretaries is due to leave shortly to have a baby.'

'Well, good luck in your quest,' Gracie said, turning the doorknob.

Before she could open the door, his hand was on her wrist. She looked up into the light grey eyes and suddenly felt dizzy. She instinctively pulled back, confused by his overwhelming masculinity.

She was close enough to feel the warmth of his hard body alongside hers and the feeling threw all her ordered thoughts into chaos.

'Would you consider filling her place?' he asked, staring down at her, the grey eyes flicking insistently across her face. 'You're an experienced secretary. Jennifer told me that some time ago, in passing. There would be no problem getting a work permit, and you'll be close to your sister until she's fully recovered.'

His proposal had so taken her by surprise that Gracie gazed up at him in silence, before the full impact of what he was saying sank in.

'I already have a job in England, Mr Drake,' she said shakily.

'Leave it.'

'I can't just leave my job, my flat, my friends, just at the drop of a hat!'

'Why not?'

'Because, because . . .' She tried to think of a few valid reasons but was finding it difficult. 'Because I just can't,' she finished limply.

'Scared?'

'No!' She glared up at him, annoyed to see that he was looking at her with amusement, and she again had the peculiar feeling that he could see into the workings of her mind as clearly as if she had written out her thoughts on a blackboard.

'What, then?' he asked softly. 'It'll be a challenge. You have no family in England. I admit your flat's there, and I'll see to it that someone respectable is found to rent it in your absence. Or else my company will cover the rent ourselves. As to friends, you can make new ones over here. We Americans are really quite nice people, if you give us a chance. So where's the problem?'

'The problem, Mr Drake,' Gracie said, emphasising his name coldly, 'is that I don't like having my life manoeuvred by someone else.'

'You allowed yourself to be manoeuvred by your sister into dropping everything you were doing and rushing across the Atlantic to sort her problems out for her.' His voice was disarmingly mild, but with the certainty of someone who knew that they were blocking over every chance of escape. 'Think about it,' he said, releasing her wrist and standing back. 'After all, I have no intention of prosecuting your sister, but there is always the matter of the Ferrari...'

'I hope you don't think you can blackmail me into staying here!' Gracie exclaimed.

'Who, me? Of course not. I like to think of it as persuasion.'

'Well, I'll give your offer some thought, Mr Drake.' Gracie had half opened the door and was prepared to step outside.

'Good. I'll meet you tomorrow for lunch. Twelve-thirty. Zantini's restaurant in Greenwich Village, just off West Fourth Street. We can discuss your decision.' He smiled and for a second Gracie felt like someone desperately struggling in deep waters, trying to relocate some foothold of reason and sanity which seemed to have deserted her.

She spent the rest of the day, and most of the night as well, trying to find reasons for not accepting his offer. She didn't like the way that he had thrown it at her. More perplexing was why he was so insistent that she work for him. It could only be that he still harboured some plan to coerce her into breaking up her sister's relationship with Rickie. Did it really matter that much to him?

Still, whatever the reasons, the thought was tempting. Over the past sixteen months, her life had settled into a rut. Collins and Collins, where she worked, recognised her talents but had explained to her that they could not promote her into anything more interesting for at least another year, primarily because of the smallness of their firm.

Gracie ate an early dinner and retired to bed with a book, which she abandoned after ten minutes. Her head was too full of possibilities. By the time she began drifting into sleep, she had already made her decision, and she drily thought that it had come as no surprise.

CHAPTER TWO

GRACIE had a shrewd idea that her sister was not going to be overly impressed with her suggestion to take up Morgan's offer of a job.

She mulled over the potential problems as she dressed the following morning, carefully picking the least ordinary of her clothes from the scant wardrobe that she had brought over.

She had decided that she would go to the hospital first thing, and then on to meet Morgan at the restaurant, timing it so that she would arrive on the dot of twelve-thirty if not slightly before. Gracie had never viewed unpunctuality as a desirable trait, and she certainly had no intention of making a belated entrance after he was seated at the table, not in the dull patterned skirt and cream top which she was wearing. She could just imagine the light grey eyes flicking over her in amusement as he absorbed the very ordinary image that she presented. The mere thought made her cringe in embarrassment.

Jenny was wearing a sullen, bored expression when Gracie entered the room. She had never liked being cooped up in one place for too long. The prospect of enforced inactivity for two months must, Gracie thought, already be beginning to take its toll.

She chatted amiably for a few minutes, watching the expression on Jenny's face lighten when she was handed the magazines that Gracie had brought for her, then she said tentatively, 'As you won't be able to go back to work for a while yet, Mr Drake has offered me a job as one of his personal assistants.'

'He what?'

'He offered me a job.'

'Are you going to accept?' As she had expected, Jenny did not sound wildly keen on the idea.

'I think so. It'll give me the opportunity to be here with you while you're recovering, and besides, it might be interesting. I was getting a little fed up working for Mr Collins. This might be just the sort of break I've been looking for.'

She looked at her sister calmly, almost hearing the clicking of her mind as it digested this bit of news and worked out what it would mean for her.

'I only wanted you to speak with him,' Jenny protested, 'to ask him not to take any action over you know what, the car, and to let me remain in New York. Not to start angling for my job.'

'It's not your job,' Gracie said brightly. 'You can have that as soon as you're well enough to get back to work. And he won't be taking you to court over the accident.' Even though, she thought, he would have every right to.

'Well, that's something.' Jenny eyed her warily through her long eyelashes. 'It's just that I've been enjoying my freedom over here. I don't want you to be constantly hovering over me, lecturing me on everything I do.'

'There's a limit to what you can get up to in a hospital room,' Gracie pointed out. She didn't want to add that that was the main reason that she had agreed to the offer. She would have the best of both worlds: she would be in the same place as Jenny, just in case she really did need some help or started hollering for attention when the boredom set in, and she would not have the problem of having to wonder constantly what her sister was getting up to.

'Did Morgan tell you about Rickie?'

'We skirted over the subject.'

'I suppose he wants you to talk me out of seeing him. He doesn't seem to realise that Rickie's old enough to take care of himself.'

Gracie was in no mood to become embroiled in her sister's arguments. Not right now. She knew that if she gave any indication that she disapproved of their relationship Jenny would immediately start up a defensive argument that could last until the cows came home.

'What's Mr Drake like to work for?' she asked, changing the subject.

'I was training under his principal secretary. But he seemed reasonable enough whenever I met him. Until, that is, Rickie and I started seeing each other.'

She swept her fingers through her long, honey-gold hair, twirling it into an attractive pile on the top of her head. The movement was smooth and done with conscious grace, and Gracie wondered whether it had been added to her sister's little reservoir of gestures which she did almost unconsciously, and always to draw attention to herself.

'I'm meeting him at midday at some restaurant called Zantini's to discuss terms of the contract.'

'Zantini's? He must be keen to have you.' Jenny grinned and threw her sister a calculating, knowing look which Gracie disregarded. 'Well, I guess it'll be quite nice having you over here. What with me being in hospital and everything. You can bring me chocolates and magazines.'

'Chocolates? You'll never eat them,' Gracie said, and Jenny giggled in agreement. She had always watched her weight carefully.

Now that she had broken the news to her sister, Gracie's mind was racing ahead, anticipating the luncheon date with Morgan. She was surprised when she bent forward to kiss her sister goodbye and Jenny's arms twined round her neck.

'This time it's the real thing, Gracie,' she whispered with a little catch in her voice. 'You have to take my side.'

Gracie hugged her back, not pursuing the subject, but later on, as she made her way to Greenwich Village, she kept going over in her mind what Jenny had said to her.

There had been a sort of urgent pleading in her voice that Gracie had never recognised before. In the past Jenny had always been in total control of her love-life. Now, Gracie got the feeling that emotions were calling the shots, and she wondered whether this was more than simply a passing crush.

It was quarter to one by the time she finally made it to the restaurant. Morgan was waiting for her at the table, and he stood up when she approached, reaching out to shake her hand. He had strong hands, long-fingered and sure. He was wearing a charcoal-grey suit and looked disconcertingly elegant and businesslike.

If Gracie had expected his appeal to have diminished overnight, she realised with dismay that it had been a misplaced hope. He was as aggressively sexual as she had feared. As his hand grasped hers, she felt a quiver of alarm rush through her. You're a fool, she told herself scornfully. This man was born to conquer beautiful women, women with exquisite dress sense and the well coiffured look that breathes sophistication.

Out of the corner of her eye, Gracie saw two such women at one of the adjacent tables looking at him with interest, and she wondered whether he always elicited that sort of reaction from the opposite sex.

She thought it just as well that she could appreciate his physical attractiveness while remaining immune to its effect. Hadn't she always been able to stand back and let her head handle her relationships with men, instead of her heart?

'What would you like to drink?' he asked, as they sat down and a waiter appeared with two menus.

'Perrier water, please.'

'Non-drinker?'

'Only when I think I may need a clear head,' Gracie replied truthfully, thinking that in the company of this man a clear head was the most important thing anyone could have. He laughed as though he had read what she had been thinking and ordered a bourbon for himself.

Gracie had expected him to ask her immediately whether she had accepted his offer, but while they ate he angled the conversation round to herself, and her job in England. Did she like her job? London? Did she frequent the theatre? He had a curious talent for appearing genuinely interested in everything she was saying.

Probably just a show, she thought half-heartedly. Besides, did it matter what sort of impression she gave him? It was hardly as though she was being interviewed for a job that she specifically wanted. If he changed his mind about her, then it would be no hardship.

Over her entrée of superbly cooked fillet steak in mustard and brandy, Gracie surreptitiously studied the hard contours of his face. He had the bearing of someone born to wield power. When he smiled, it softened his features, but the watchfulness in his eyes was always there. It was hardly surprising that he had carved his way through the cut-throat world of big business with such apparent ease. She suspected that he possessed a core of hardness that made him a formidable opponent.

Over coffee, he asked her with no preliminary warning, 'Have you made your mind up on my offer?'

He sat back in his chair with his arms folded across his chest, and looked at her narrowly from under his thick black lashes.

'Will you tell me a bit more about what the job will entail?'

She listened while he briefed her on the duties involved, answering her questions with precision and clarity.

Gracie nodded and thought that if she had had any doubts lingering, they would have by now been demolished. The job sounded fascinating. It would involve far more responsibility than she currently had working at Collins and Collins, and there was every indication that she would be encouraged to expand her knowledge of business affairs to the maximum.

'I'm prepared to double whatever salary you're getting at the moment in England,' he said when there was a break to her questions.

'Why?' Gracie sipped a mouthful of coffee and looked at him curiously.

'Because I want you, and I'm prepared to pay.'

She felt a little stab of pleasure and lowered her eyes hurriedly.

'So is it yes or no?'

'I accept.' He didn't look surprised; perhaps he was accustomed to having his own way in whatever he wanted, and she continued quickly, 'But I shall have to return to London so that I can sort myself out and arrange the leasing of my flat. Also, I'll have to talk to my boss and we'll have to work out what can be done about working my month's notice out.'

Morgan nodded, then he said suddenly, 'I intend to be in London myself in a week's time. I'll meet you and we can travel back together. I can begin briefing you on my business concerns over here.'

Gracie felt a peculiar quiver of alarm. It was one thing working with Morgan Drake, but it was quite another to be with him out of a business environment. She knew that instinctively, even though there was no rational basis to her assumption.

Not, she thought, that it would make a scrap of difference. He was an intensely attractive man, but not the sort that would be interested in her at all. A woman would have to be very beautiful to hold his attention, and she was anything but that.

She nodded slowly, pushing any awkward thoughts out of her head.

'When do you want to fly?' he asked. 'I'll book your ticket for you.'

'I already have a return ticket. Perhaps I can just get the date changed. Although...' she frowned '...it was a cheap deal. Maybe——'

'Forget about all that, I'll get you a new ticket.' He beckoned the waiter over for the bill, and Gracie got the impression that the subject had been dismissed as far as he was concerned.

'Where are you staying?' he asked, scanning the bill quickly and then dropping his credit card on to the silver tray.

'Why?'

'I need an address so that I can send the ticket there. Do you normally ask so many questions?'

'Must be a habit that I've acquired from having spent so many years trying to look after Jenny.' She gave him the address of her hotel and he nodded, but didn't write it down.

He was looking at her curiously, and Gracie suddenly had the impression that he was again making comparisons between Jenny and herself. She felt herself redden. For perhaps the first time since they had sat down to lunch, the hard grey eyes were sizing her up as a woman, rather than as a potential employee, assessing the slight frame, the delicate features, the unexciting straight chestnut hair parted in the centre and falling in a clear sweep to her shoulders.

'Your clothes don't do much for you,' he said suddenly, and his eyes rested on her in a rather franker assessment. 'You're thin, but not that thin. You ought to steer clear of shirts and dresses that cover you up.'

He studied her coolly, tapping his credit card, which the waiter had returned to him, against the face of his wallet.

Gracie wanted to say: well, I suppose you'd know all about clothes; but his personal remark had caught her off guard and she couldn't think of anything sensible to say.

'I don't see what my taste in dress has to do with you,' she finally said in a sarcastic voice, making it clear that she resented his intrusion into her personal taste.

'On the contrary. Now that you're about to work for me, every last detail of your physical appearance will be my business.' He shot her a veiled, mocking glance. 'You'll be on show a lot of the time. You'll be surprised at exactly how important clothes will become. We can do some shopping when I'm in London before we return to New York.'

'No, thank you,' Gracie replied politely. He might be able to dictate to his other secretaries, and his women—and she was sure there was no shortage of those—what they wore and when, but she was damned if she was going to allow it. Besides, she had no intention of wasting what was left of her savings on a lavish spending spree. What if she burnt her boats, came to New York and found that she hated it?

'We'll see,' he murmured speculatively, and Gracie was forcibly struck by the impression he gave of being a man who always got exactly what he wanted. When he offered her a ride back to her hotel in the plush limousine which was waiting outside for him, she shook her head, insisting that she preferred to make her own way back so that she could appreciate the unfamiliarity of the environment.

She watched the air-conditioned car sift into the stream of yellow cabs and expelled a sigh of relief.

When she was in his presence she could not seem to think in her normal orderly manner. Now she allowed her mind to ramble freely over the pros and cons of her decision to work with him. There were some things that she didn't like about him. She didn't care for his unspoken assumption that he could have whatever he wanted. It showed how his mind worked, and it showed that beneath the charm there was a streak of steely arrogance that was only barely concealed.

She also had not cared for his comments on her appearance, even though she granted that he might have a point. She was strolling past one of the larger department stores and automatically peered into the window, seeing reflected back at her a smallish, indistinct but not unpleasant person. Perhaps she ought to buy a few new clothes, but if she did they would be conservative and in muted colours, and if he still found grounds for complaint then that was just too bad. His opinions didn't really matter anyway.

She didn't see Morgan again before she left New York. She received a first-class return ticket to Heathrow the following morning, with a typed note giving her details of whom she should contact within the company to finalise the details of her contract. By the end of the week, Gracie had signed over herself to a completely new career path.

'I hope you know what you're doing,' Jenny said to her the evening before Gracie was due to leave. Rickie had just visited her, bringing with him a mass of wild flowers and a pale pink silk dressing-gown, and she was in high spirits.

'I'm not travelling to Mars,' Gracie protested. 'Besides, what have I got to lose? I'm twenty-five and I'm just taking a break from the rut that I've been in for the past few years.'

'Well, just so long as you don't start acting the elder sister with me when I'm out of hospital.'

'I *am* your elder sister,' Gracie reminded her gently. 'Is it any wonder that I worry about you? Besides, you can show off your new conquest to me.' She knew that that would divert her, and it did. She spent the next thirty minutes listening to her sister chat about Rickie, and allowed her mind to wander over what she would have to do over the next ten days before she flew back to New York.

Things moved with surprising speed when she returned to London. Mr Collins told her that he would be sorry to see her go, that hard-working young people were difficult to find; and in view of the special circumstances attached to her new job he released her from working out her one month's notice with benevolent resignation.

She arranged to rent out her flat almost overnight. She placed an advert in a London weekly the day after she arrived, and the following evening had interviewed and accepted two young accountancy students as tenants. It was almost the easiest part of leaving London. Pleasant flats for rent were like gold dust and there was no shortage of prospective candidates for the vacancy.

By the time her short stay was nearing its end, Gracie could hardly contain the rising excitement inside her. She had packed up all the clothes that she intended to take over, and was sitting on one of her cases, idly going over in her mind whether she had done everything that needed doing, when the doorbell sounded.

She stood up abruptly, watching in dismay as the lid of the old suitcase flapped open now that there was no pressure on it to keep it closed. She would have to do something about that—perhaps tie some string around it, or else some makeshift straps.

It had not occurred to her to buy new suitcases. In fact, she had so rarely used them in the past that she had forgotten exactly how decrepit they were, and by the time she realised that they would only function with a lot of additional gadgets it had been too late in the day to rush out and purchase more, if she could have been bothered.

She pulled open the door, expecting it to be her neighbour who had promised to come over for a last cup of coffee. Morgan was standing outside. Gracie's startled eyes took in the tall, muscular frame and the amused grey eyes.

'Hello,' she said, flushing as she realised what sort of picture she must present in her faded denims and old white T-shirt carelessly tucked into the waistband. 'What on earth are you doing here?'

'Is that all the enthusiasm you can muster for your future boss? Aren't you going to invite me in?' He leaned against the door-frame and looked down at her with infuriating amusement.

Gracie stepped aside to let him pass. It irritated her for some reason to see how he dwarfed the small flat, leisurely looking around at the sparse furnishings. She had removed most of her treasured objects, storing them in two large crates in her locker in the basement of the building. What remained were the bare essentials, which made the place look almost more naked than if everything had been taken out.

'What are you doing here?' she repeated, shutting the door loudly and marching behind him.

'Have you forgotten? We have a date, of sorts.'

Gracie stared at him with a puzzled expression on her face, which gradually cleared as she remembered his threat to take her shopping.

She was still angry and taken aback at his presence in her flat and was finding it difficult to think clearly. He was standing by the window, facing her, one hand stuck into a trouser pocket, the other absently fingering one of the leaves on her tall Swiss cheese plant. The sun, pouring in through the window, made him seem even darker and taller than she remembered.

He really was impressive, she thought reluctantly. Broad-shouldered, slim-hipped, with long legs that looked as though they belonged to an athlete and not to a successful businessman.

'I'm sorry,' she said, not feeling in the least bit sorry. 'I had completely forgotten, and it's really too late now. There are a few last-minute things I want to get done before tomorrow, so...' She let her words trail off meaningfully.

She wished he would not look at her quite so carefully. She felt at a disadvantage enough as it was, in her casual, stay-at-home clothes. If he had been sceptical of her taste in dress before, then he must now be looking at her with profound disdain.

'What few last-minute things do you have to do?' he asked, resuming his prowling inspection of the room.

'Things,' Gracie replied irritably. 'I have to tidy up a bit, clean the fridge out. I don't want to leave the place looking as if it's been hit by a bomb.'

'You can do all that this evening. Right now you're coming with me to Harrods.'

'I can't afford to buy a handkerchief from Harrods, far less a wardrobe of clothes!' Gracie folded her arms across her breasts and glared at him.

'I'll pay. Call it a clothing allowance.'

'I'm not accepting money from you for clothes!' she exclaimed angrily, drawing back slightly as he approached her.

'You're wasting your time arguing the point,' he said in a lazy voice, 'and now that you work for me I'd be grateful for a little less self-righteous anger. Do you realise what other people would think if they could hear you now?'

'They would think that I didn't want you to buy my clothes for me!'

'They would think that we were lovers, because dutiful secretaries never raise their voices when addressing their boss.'

Gracie's eyes widened. She could feel her face turning bright red as she took in the implications of what he was saying. How could she tell him that she normally never raised her voice, but that there was something alarming about him that seemed to provoke all the wrong reactions in her?

After spending years looking after Jenny, she had learned to keep a tight rein over her temper, but Morgan bothered her and she wasn't too sure why.

'I'll see if I can fish something out of one of the suitcases,' she conceded quietly. 'I hadn't planned on going anywhere today and, apart from what I'll be travelling in, everything else is packed.'

'Come as you are. You look . . . charming.'

He looked her up and down, quickly but expertly, and Gracie wanted to hit him because he was being patronising. Instead she snatched up her bag which was lying on the sofa and checked to make sure that the house keys were safely tucked inside.

She had automatically thought that they would take the Underground, but there was a taxi waiting outside for them and he steered her inside. He must have been complacently assured that he would succeed in getting her to come out with him.

'So tell me a little bit about yourself,' he said as the taxi pulled away from the kerb. 'How long have you lived in London?'

'Since my parents died,' Gracie replied. 'Gracious, aren't the streets packed with people? It must be the sudden burst of hot weather. London always seems too small to cope with tourists and Londoners all out of doors at the same time.'

She peered through the window of the taxi, feeling his sideways glance on her face as he registered her change of conversation, but he didn't say anything, instead falling into line with her and chatting superficially about places to see and visit in London.

All the while, Gracie could feel his warm presence next to her and it was disturbing. She had never been given to bursts of wild infatuation for the opposite sex, and had certainly never been as aware of a man as she was of him.

She could feel the fine hairs on her arm almost standing on end and made a deliberate effort to keep her eyes diverted from his strong, sharp profile. The last thing she needed at this stage in the game was to find herself having a crush on the man she would be working for, especially a man whose sex appeal was as blatantly obvious as his was, and who was probably fully aware of the effect that he had on women.

How could he fail to be? As they walked through Harrods she was aware of heads turning, eyes covertly assessing the man at her side, and probably also speculating on what he was doing in the company of a very plain girl in jeans and white cotton T-shirt. The whole thing probably afforded him a great deal of inner amusement.

She had been determined to make the shopping expedition as short as possible, but that turned out to be more difficult than she had anticipated.

Morgan eyed the clothes on the racks fleetingly, but with an uncanny and almost professional knowledge of what would suit her. He picked out colours that she would never have dreamt of choosing for herself, and as she tried on the various outfits she was surprised at how they flattered her fine-boned face and figure.

'You obviously have some experience of this,' she admitted reluctantly.

'A compliment of sorts,' he asked in a mocking, incredulous voice, 'from my cool-headed little secretary?'

'If you choose to look at it like that,' Gracie snapped.

He nodded to the sales assistant to add the figure-hugging burgundy dress which Gracie had just tried on to the rest of the clothes which he intended to purchase, and which had been neatly folded with tissue paper and stacked. She hoped it would be the last of the outfits. She didn't dare to think what they would cost.

'Well,' he leant forward to whisper in her ear, 'if you must know, I'm quite *au fait* with *haute couture*. Comes from always having the dubious pleasure of going out with very expensive ladies.'

'Well,' Gracie said staring up at him, and with admirable composure, 'what a little treat for you to be shopping for an inexpensive one.' She regretted saying it the minute the words were out because he looked at her with a mocking smile, and she wondered whether he had translated her words into meaning that she placed herself into the category of his women. Too late. She had said it, and she immediately turned away to hide her confusion.

'Now,' he said, 'do you have anything dressy?'

'Why would I be needing something dressy?'

'A simple yes or no answer will do fine.' He looked at her with one arched eyebrow, his head slightly tilted to one side. She thought that he would have made a superb barrister. There was something about his eyes and his manner of speech which implied that he would not let anything rest until he had seen it through to its natural conclusion, or at least until he felt that he had sufficiently exhausted the subject.

'No,' Gracie admitted grudgingly, 'I don't suppose so.' Her line of clothes tended to be functional and comfortable, and certainly did not include anything remotely resembling the sort of evening wear which she assumed he had in mind.

Before she could open her mouth to protest, he had ushered her across to the rack of designer evening dresses and was flicking through them with his hand. He pulled out a deep red one which Gracie was appalled to see was so tiny that it looked as though it had been shrunk ten times over in the wash.

'I can't possibly wear that,' she said firmly.

'Let me see you in it.'

She looked at him furiously, but the sales assistant had approached them, and it was just not in her character to create a scene in public. She had always avoided drawing attention to herself, and she did not intend to break the habit now, least of all in the middle of the crowded fashion floor in Harrods.

She gritted her teeth together and went into the dressing-room, wriggling into the dress and then standing back to see whether it looked as awful as it had felt putting on.

It didn't. It moulded itself to her curves like elastic, and even managed to show up a few which she had not known even existed.

She expected Morgan to grin in triumph when she stepped outside the changing-room, but he didn't. He stood back and scrutinised her in total silence.

'Fine,' he said abruptly to the salesgirl, 'we'll take that as well,' then he turned away and began walking towards the pay counter.

Gracie contorted her body out of the dress and then joined him. His reaction had puzzled her, and she put it down to tiredness. She was feeling quite exhausted herself. They had been in the store for over two and a half hours and her arms were killing her from getting into outfits and then getting out of them again.

Did Jenny go through all this every time she chose a dress? Gracie watched as Morgan paid the bill, then tentatively broached the subject of paying him back as they struggled out of the shop with their arms laden with shopping bags.

'I told you,' he said curtly as they stepped into a taxi, 'they'll come under company expenses. If it makes you feel any easier, my last secretary had a dress allowance, and she certainly didn't spend her time trying to argue her way out of accepting it.'

Gracie didn't really care if he had made that up for her benefit, because it made her feel easier. She closed her eyes and settled back against the seat, her body feeling as limp as a sponge. She thought that she would miss London with its black, high-domed taxis and old grey buildings. It possessed a certain genteel charm which New York lacked. New York was too fast and too tall to be really charming.

When the taxi stopped in front of her block of flats, Gracie's eyes flew open and she sat upright.

'I would offer you coffee,' she began, 'but the remnants of what I had have gone the way of all the other perishables. In the bin.'

'No problem. I have to get back now anyway. I'll see you tomorrow at the airport.' He reached across her and snapped open the door, and for one confusing moment

Gracie's head was filled with the sheer electricity that seemed to emanate from his body.

She gathered up her bags, refusing his offer to help her with them up to the flat, and hurried up to her front door as fast as her legs would take her.

Once she was inside her flat, she dropped the bags on the floor and slumped down on the sofa. She didn't quite understand what Morgan Drake was doing to her, but she understood it well enough to know that she didn't like it. When she was sitting next to him on the plane she would have to make sure that she ignored the fact that he was a man, and concentrate on the fact that he was her employer.

She looked around her and tried to imagine what it would be like not coming back to this tiny flat every evening after work. It was staggering to think that an eight-hour plane flight would be one of the most major dividing lines in her entire life.

She could feel herself on the brink of becoming maudlin, and promptly squashed the sensation by inspecting all her purchases one by one and then packing them in the emptiest of the three suitcases.

There would be time enough to miss London when she was in New York. A flat had already been arranged for her. They told her that it was in the same block that housed Jenny's, but that meant nothing to her since she had not been to her sister's flat. With disarming nonchalance, Jenny had lent it for the last month to a friend of hers and her very young child, on the grounds that she was almost always over at Rickie's place, which was why Gracie had wisely opted for staying in a reasonable hotel while she was in New York, where at least she would be private.

As Morgan had predicted, all those last-minute things that needed doing were accomplished in under an hour, and with time on her hands Gracie sat at her living-room bay window, alternately reading and staring out on to the street below, as the sun became dimmer and dimmer, and finally dipped down altogether.

She felt that everything was moving fast, too fast. Her life, which had been so neatly wrapped and packaged, was now flung open—and her emotions...? They seemed to be moving too fast as well. Though, she thought dimly, not too fast for me to handle.

CHAPTER THREE

JENNY was recuperating quickly. Gracie could tell because over the past three weeks since she had returned to New York she had been visiting the hospital on a more regular basis, and was having to contend with her sister's increasing frustration at not being outdoors to enjoy the splendid summer weather.

The sulky expression which Jenny adopted whenever she was bored was more pronounced, and Gracie was glad that she was cooped up, because that particular brand of sulkiness always heralded something reckless.

'It's all right for you,' she had complained the previous day, 'you can spend all the time you want lounging around in the sunshine. I can only lie here and think about it! Not,' she continued coyly, 'that you seem to want to do much lounging around. For heaven's sake, Gracie, you spend half your time working! Even when you don't have to!'

Gracie had not been able to deny it. She really did seem to spend most of her waking time at work, enjoying every minute of her demanding job. Morgan had been true to his word, and in a matter of days rather than months she had been allocated responsibility little by little; each gradual and additional responsibility had anchored her ever more firmly into her work.

Somewhere in the dim recesses of her mind she asked herself whether the mere fact of being near Morgan had anything to do with her willingness to work continually overtime, but it was a question which she had become adept at avoiding the minute it wriggled uncomfortably into her consciousness. She told herself that his presence was only invigorating in so far as he seemed to emit a constant charge of high-powered energy, which not only she but everyone else found electrically motivating.

It was all so different from the slow-moving pace at Collins and Collins, where decisions were jointly discussed and re-discussed, and finally acted upon in a leisurely and unhurried manner.

Morgan, she had discovered from almost the first day, was a man who seemed to feed on the merciless cut and thrust of the business world, possessing an almost uncanny knack of making swift and accurate decisions and always keeping just that one step ahead of the ever-changing stock market.

His formidable aggression permeated through the entire company. How, she thought, could she be expected to be exempt? She worked in such close proximity to him that of course it was bound to rub off on her, to fill her with an enthusiasm for work which she had never before in her life experienced.

She was finishing for the day, scanning the reports which she had inputted on to the word processor, and preparing for another long and patient visit to the hospital, when her buzzer sounded and the security guard on the downstairs desk said, 'Miss Jackson is here to see Mr Drake.'

'Who is Miss Jackson, Harry?' Gracie asked with a puzzled frown. She cast her eyes down her appointment book and, as she expected, could see no entry under the name of Miss Jackson, or Miss anything for that matter.

'One of Mr Drake's ladies.'

Well, wasn't it about time that one of Morgan's female following reared her head? She was fully aware of the fact that he played as hard as he worked, but she had never seen, far less met any of his women, and she had gathered that he viewed the working environment as something sacrosanct. Like a lot of powerful and successful men, he did not like mixing business with pleasure, and so far it had worked.

'Allow her up, Harry,' Gracie said, dimly hearing in the background a female voice saying that too damn right she had to be allowed up; did he *really* think she was a security risk, for heaven's sake?

She wondered whether she ought to stay or not, when the decision was taken out of her hands by the door bursting open.

The woman who swept in could have stepped right off the cover of *Vogue*. She was tall, sleek, and very expensive-looking, and she made Gracie feel instantly dull in comparison.

'I'm here to see your boss,' the woman said, throwing Gracie a bored look that seemed to imply that she was looking at someone particularly uninteresting.

Gracie called Morgan on the internal line and said, 'There's a Miss Jackson here to see you.'

She heard him swear softly under his breath, then he said, 'Can't you get rid of her somehow? I'm busy. You know I still have all those reports on the Derekson take-over to look through.'

'Shall I show her in, then?'

'You can wipe that sugar-sweet smile off your face,' he muttered, clearly hearing her amusement down the line and not liking it, 'and show her in if you must. But don't leave. This visit is going to be brief and I want to see you afterwards.'

She heard the abrupt slam of the receiver, and said politely, 'If you'd care to follow me?'

How on earth did some women manage to look so perfectly groomed at six o'clock on a hot summer evening? Every strand of hair was in place, the make-up carefully applied and not looking in the least bit jaded, the lip-gloss still wet and gleaming, as though it had been put on only a few minutes before. Perhaps it had been.

When Gracie opened the door, Miss Jackson swept past her in a cloud of fragrant perfume, and said, 'Morgan, darling! I know you don't like me disturbing you at work, but I just *had* to see you.' She shut the door very firmly behind her, and Gracie grimaced.

It didn't take a great deal of imagination to work out what this little impulsive visit was a prelude to. An amorous kiss over the desk, a few inviting phrases, a ride down in the lift, then who knew? Gracie found herself picturing the scene, and immediately shoved it to the back of her mind, not caring for it at all.

She started sifting some of her files into order, but taking her time and hoping that she wouldn't still be standing around in an hour's time. Why did he want her to stay anyway? Did he think that if he ran into any trouble and started yelling for help she would be conveniently placed to rush in and rescue him? The thought was quite amusing, and she chuckled.

She could imagine that the elegant Miss Jackson could be very persistent if she wanted, and Gracie had gathered from some of Morgan's throwaway remarks over the past few weeks that persistence was not a personal trait he found very endearing in his women.

Jenny had told her that he attracted women like flies, even though she couldn't quite understand it, as he didn't seem to be a fun type at all. Gracie had interpreted that remark to mean that Morgan did not like clubs and the bright lights, nor did he like flirting with young girls, even though the young girls might be very pretty ones.

'There's always a new girl in his company, about every four weeks or so,' Jenny had said. 'You can tell because it always seems to be reported in the gossip columns.'

Gracie stared at the closed door and wondered how long Miss Jackson had been on the scene. Longer than four weeks, she would have imagined, if she felt comfortable enough to swoop into his office, even if it was after normal working hours.

She finished the filing and told herself that what Morgan Drake did in his personal life was no concern of hers.

Nevertheless she felt her stomach muscles tighten when the black, adjoining door opened and they both emerged, Miss Jackson clinging possessively to Morgan's arm, in a very chic, very confident and very *haute couture* manner.

'May I leave now, Mr Drake?' Gracie asked, pointedly glancing at her watch.

'I said I had a few things to say to you, and I still have.' He looked down at the swaying redhead on his arm, and said in a low voice, 'I still have some work to do. I'll call you later.'

'Promise?' she asked teasingly, her lips pouting. 'Sure your little secretary person will let you? She seems a touch possessive.' Before he could answer she drew his head forward with her hand and gave him a long and uninhibited kiss.

Wonderful, Gracie thought, inwardly cringing at being described as a 'little secretary person'. Nothing like playing a little hard to get, was there? Although on reflection, if the average lifespan of one of his women was a month, then he probably preferred to avoid the time-consuming game of enticing an over-coy lady into bed.

The thought was so uncharitable that Gracie busied herself slotting her pens into her drawer, only looking up when the redhead disappeared through the door with a fluting, 'Bye bye!'

As soon as the door had closed behind her, Morgan turned to Gracie with a dark expression on his face.

'Why did you let her up here?' he demanded, thrusting his hands into his pockets. His eyes were slate-hard, and there was an element of accusation in them that infuriated Gracie.

'What was I supposed to do?' she asked calmly. 'Have her declared a health risk and tossed out of the building?'

'I can do without your sarcasm,' he said softly. 'You could have told her that I wasn't in.'

He stared at her broodingly.

When she didn't answer, Morgan picked up the fountain pen lying on her desk and began twirling it between his fingers. The silence stretched between them, broken only by the shuffling sounds of Gracie's clearing up.

She had no intention of getting caught up in his little affairs, and even less intention of deflecting his pursuers by lying to them. As far as she was concerned, if he managed to get himself involved with women who wanted more out of the relationship than he was prepared to give, then that was his look out. He would have to call on his own resources to fend them off.

'Well?' he persisted, dropping the pen on the desk and looking at her intently through narrowed eyes.

'Well what?'

'Stop trying to avoid the subject. I don't like women coming into my office. It's a part of my life that has nothing to do with them. If Alex shows up again, perhaps you could make that clear.'

'Alex?'

'Miss Jackson.'

Gracie nodded slowly, feeling the anger bubbling inside her like a tiny active volcano waiting to explode.

'I gather you don't approve?'

Gracie looked at him coolly. 'It's not a question of whether I approve or disapprove of what you do outside work, Mr Drake, or with whom. I'm just saying that I don't think it's my place to provide alibis for you when you've become bored with your latest possession and you no longer want her around.'

He flushed a dull red. She could tell that he was angry, but she didn't care. He was right. She didn't approve of his approach to women, and she was not going to be party to it.

'Oh, for heaven's sake, it's hardly something to get so worked up about, little secretary person,' he added teasingly.

Gracie flushed. 'I beg to differ,' she replied coldly. 'Now, is that all? Is it all right if I leave?'

Maybe, she thought, she was being pedantic. Or maybe—and she pushed this thought out of her head as soon as it entered—she just did not like to see him flaunting other women in front of her. Especially women who thought that good manners were not a social requisite. She wondered whether it was simply good old-fashioned jealousy in the face of physical perfection, or, worse, good old-fashioned jealousy because they were going out, dating, sleeping with Morgan Drake.

The thought made her mouth go suddenly sour, and she quickly rescued her bag from the swivel chair, slinging it over her shoulder.

'I'll walk down with you,' he said, falling into step next to her. When he gently steered her into the lift, with his hand under her elbow, she could almost feel her body tense.

Things were fine as long as he wasn't near her, but the minute he got close she felt her pulses begin to race as though her body could not help but react to his masculinity, despite what her head told it to do.

She was about to walk off in the opposite direction as they reached the downstairs foyer when he asked her whether she would like to have a drink with him.

It was the first time he had done this since she had begun working for him. Normally, he was still at his desk when she left in the evening, and she knew that he kept regularly late hours.

'I want to talk to you about Rickie and your sister,' he said, seeing her hesitancy, 'so don't look so anxious. This isn't a proposition. I'm not going to suddenly lunge at you in a crowded bar and have my wicked way.'

He was watching her face as he said this, and Gracie flushed. Not because she had been thinking along those lines—she had known from the very first moment they had met that she was not in his league at all—but because his words had evoked a very graphic picture of what it must be like to make love with him.

'Yes, all right,' she said hurriedly. 'I was planning on going to the hospital, but Jenny won't mind too much if I don't come this evening.'

Outside, the air was heavy and hot. Gracie had noticed since she had been here that summer in New York brought days that seemed much stiller and warmer than in London.

At lunchtime, when she went outside, there were always countless people sitting on benches, feeding pigeons, or simply walking about with their sleeves rolled up eating ices, and their movements always seemed to be lethargic and weighty, as though the incredible heat had forced them down into their lowest gear.

She was the same. She would wear light cotton suits, several of which she had bought at some of the large department stores in New York, but after half an hour in the sun she would return to her office bathed in a fine film of perspiration, and thankful for the cool reprieve of the air-conditioning.

They walked through the still crowded streets to a small wine bar which was popular with the businessmen in the nearby office buildings. Gracie had been there a couple of times before with one of the girls from work, and she liked it. It was nothing like an English pub, it lacked that dark, intimate atmosphere, but there was something airy and hi-tech about it that somehow blended well with the similarly airy and hi-tech buildings around it. It was tasteful but impersonal, and catered for the fast-moving New York crowd.

When they were seated at one of the circular metal tables with their drinks in front of them Morgan leaned back against his chair, loosening the knot of his tie in short, jerky movements.

'I've spoken to Rickie about Jennifer,' he said, sipping from his drink, 'and he won't listen to reason. He's young, he's besotted and he doesn't even want to hear me mention the word "responsibility" in connection with the company. I need to know what sort of impression your sister's given you about their relationship.'

'Why?'

'That's one habit you haven't shed since you've been over here,' Morgan said drily, and when Gracie asked what that was he replied, with a mocking drawl, 'Your curiosity, your ability to answer nearly everything with a question.'

He threw her a smile that was unconsciously sexy and charming, and Gracie nearly choked on her white wine. Was she forgetting his taste in women? Long, lean and ultra-sophisticated, the equivalent of a tall cocktail drink.

'Jenny's very keen on your nephew, Mr Drake,' she replied honestly. 'I've never known her to be quite so enraptured with anyone, ever. I haven't tried to talk her out of it because, apart from its not really being any of my concern, I didn't think that it would do any good at all. I think things ought to run their course between them.'

'Not if that course involves Rickie packing in Drake Industries, which is more or less what he insinuated he would do if I continued trying to dissuade him from a serious relationship.'

His voice was hard and uncompromising, and he gulped down another mouthful of his drink, watching her with embarrassing thoroughness from under his thick, dark lashes.

'What do you intend to do about it?'

'I thought that I could send him on a three-month course in Paris. He'll eventually be in charge of our branch over there, so it would just be a matter of accelerating something that he would have to do anyway.'

Gracie stared at him in amazement. She had already seen how unyielding he could be in business matters. He had a shrewd, alert mind that always forestalled problems before they became too large for comfort. She admired it, but now he was extending it to more than just business matters, and that she was not nearly so sure about.

'I think that would be a big mistake,' she said quietly. She waited for him to explode, but he didn't, and she continued, 'That could have just the opposite effect. If they really are in love with each other, then there's not a great deal we can do about it, or for that matter should do about it.'

'Oh, God,' he said with a cynical curl on his lips, 'you sound like one of those eternal romantics, straight out of a Victorian novel.'

Gracie wanted to laugh. She had never considered herself anything but down-to-earth and level-headed.

'I think you're confusing having a few principles with being a romantic,' she replied lightly. The pale grey eyes skimmed over her, and there was a speculative glint in them when they finally rested on her mouth.

'And I've already seen how principle-minded you are, haven't I? You left me in no doubt whatsoever of that in the office. Has anyone ever told you that you're an unusually forthright person?'

'I'm only forthright when I'm obliged to be,' she said awkwardly, wondering why the admission made her feel miserable. She had always needed to be strong, to look after Jenny. She thought with a pang that men like Morgan Drake probably found that quality admirable, but not particularly attractive.

Oh, no. From what she had seen, and certainly from what she had heard, Morgan Drake preferred his women glamorous, not too bright, and definitely not too big on principles. She supposed that he was stressed enough at work without having his brain cells challenged outside work as well.

He leant forward, resting his elbows on his knees, so close to her that her nostrils were filled with his clean, male scent. 'You have an interesting mind, Miss Grace Temple,' he said softly. 'One day it's going to land you into trouble.' He gave her an intent stare and Gracie lowered her eyes instinctively, not quite sure why. 'I'll take your advice in this instance, Gracie, because I suspect that you're probably right. Too much pressure will have them both running off to the nearest register office, as soon as your sister is fit enough to run, that is.'

He very rarely used her first name, and the sound of it coming from his lips made her uneasy. She fidgeted slightly in her chair, preparing herself to stand up and tell him that it was time for her to go.

'I'll give you a lift back to your flat,' he said, reading her mind. When she protested, he told her firmly that it was much too hot for her to jostle on public transport, and Gracie helplessly agreed. He kept his car in the basement of the office building, and they walked back to it, chatting about harmless topics.

She glanced sideways at the strong, aggressive profile and tried to ignore the thudding feeling in her chest when she viewed the prospect of being in her flat with him. She remembered how distracted she had been when he had visited her in London, and that was weeks ago, before she had been really exposed to the full potential of his threatening sexuality.

He was right. It was luxurious being driven home in the cool comfort of his sports car, the deep plush bucket seats enfolding her in their tan leather.

The block of flats, of which hers was one, was in a first-rate location between Central Park West and Broadway, and just seconds away from the Lincoln Center and Central Park. On a Saturday morning, Gracie had got into the habit of strolling into Central Park and watching the diverse mix of people, from old and sedentary on park benches, to young and energetic, roller skating on the walkways with their portable Walkmans strapped to their waists like a part of their anatomy.

'Mind if I come in for some coffee?' Morgan asked, as she'd thought he would, when the long, silver car swished to a halt outside the building. 'It'll give this traffic time to calm down a little.'

Gracie mumbled, 'Not at all,' thinking that there was precious little she could do about him coming in when he owned the damned building in the first place, but that didn't make her feel any the more relaxed as she walked along the thickly carpeted corridor to her door, with Morgan following too closely behind her for comfort.

When they stepped in, the sun was streaming in through the large windows that overlooked the bustling streets down below, and she was struck, not for the first time, by the charm of the furnishings.

The colours in the small but comfortable sitting area were muted greens and pinks, which seemed to absorb the light and reflect it back, making the room appear uncluttered and spacious.

Two broad steps on either side led off to the kitchen area on the left and the dining area on the right, with a deep alcove adjoining the kitchen into which were slotted shelves for stereo equipment, books and the television. Gracie rarely used the television, preferring to read and listen to music after she had eaten in the evening.

She had made friends with the girl who was still occupying Jenny's flat, and her young daughter, and the Sunday before had cooked them a traditional English roast meal with all the trimmings. She decided not to mention that Jenny had lent her flat out to a friend. She didn't know whether Morgan would mind or not; she doubted it, but there was no point in tempting fate. Besides, it would mean having to explain that Jenny spent most of her free evenings at Rickie's apartment in Greenwich Village, and that definitely would be shoving a stick into a hornets' nest.

She retreated to the kitchen to make the coffee and, when she emerged, warily eyed Morgan who was sitting on the large rose-patterned sofa, his long legs stretched out in front of him. He looked like a jungle cat, relaxing after a successful hunt. Well, she thought, the world of high finance and fast business in which he prowled was a jungle of sorts, and hadn't he proved that he could tackle it with all the stealthy alertness of an animal quite accustomed to its complexities?

'I'd forgotten how pleasant these flats were,' he said, casting his eyes over the rooms.

The bedroom door, Gracie was relieved to see, was shut. She immediately told herself that she was a fool if she thought that it made the slightest scrap of difference whether it was open, shut or non-existent for that matter. She would have to try and curb that imagination of hers, or else it would end up leading her down paths that led to places far better left alone.

She perched on the chair furthest away from where he was sitting and tucked her legs under her, not caring that her skirt would be horribly rumpled when she stood up.

'Did you choose the décor yourself?' she asked politely.

She did not imagine that he would have, but it was a safe topic of conversation. She was surprised when he answered her with a slow drawl, 'Something like that.'

'You mean you decided on the colour scheme and let someone else finish off all the hard work?'

Morgan laughed. 'I was coincidentally going out with a very classy interior designer at the time. She told me how she thought it ought to be done, and I agreed.'

Gracie looked at him, and their eyes met. There was a flickering expression in the grey depths that alarmed her, but when she blinked it was gone, and she assumed that it must have been a trick of the light.

'Oh,' she said, looking down.

'Somehow these surroundings seem to suit you,' he said, his eyes roving lazily over her. 'There's something kind of appealing about the way that chair engulfs you. You look incredibly young. Younger than Jennifer. What age difference is there between you?'

'Five years.'

Gracie eyed him and hoped that he had nearly finished his cup of coffee, because if he had she had no
intention of offering him a top-up. He had a strange
talent for switching his conversation on to a personal
level without any warning. It was easier to cope with
when they were at work, because she could always bury
herself in a report or else feign intense concentration in
one of the files, but it was different here.

The nervous fluttering which she always felt in the pit
of her stomach whenever she knew that he was fixing
all his attention on her for whatever reason was making
her tense. She carefully placed her empty coffee-cup on
the small smoked-glass table next to her, and stuck her
hands underneath her thighs.

'And how long ago did your parents die?'

Gracie started to tell him that it was none of his
business, but he didn't look as though he was being nosy.
He looked interested.

'Seven years ago,' she said hesitantly, 'in a car
accident. They were driving home one night after a party
and they had a head-on collision with an oncoming lorry.
The ironic part about it was that they never drank. The
lorry driver escaped with cuts and bruises. Isn't that
always the way?'

She hadn't spoken about her parents' deaths to anyone
in a long time, and it felt curiously liberating to talk
about it now. 'We were a very close family,' she said,
speaking her thoughts out loud. 'In a way it helped that
Jenny was so young when they died. It meant that I
couldn't drown indefinitely in my grief because I had to
pick up the pieces and continue, for her sake. I had
planned to go to university, to do a course in business
studies, of all things. I had to scrap that. Instead I took
a three-month crash secretarial course and went out to
work as soon as I was able after that.'

She looked at him as if what she had just confessed to him had come as much as a surprise to her as it had to him.

'Did you regret never being able to pursue your studies?'

'I did for a while. But in the end it seemed senseless to harbour any regrets. I took the only option that I thought was open to me at the time.' She raised her chin, almost as though she was expecting him to criticise her course of action. She knew that he would not, could feel it in the short silence between them, but she was not accustomed to baring her soul to anyone. She had never even mentioned any of this to her sister.

She had been telling him the truth when she said that she didn't have any lasting regrets about not completing her education. Jenny could be difficult, but Gracie loved her fiercely. There was no way that she could ever have sacrificed her upbringing for the sake of a three-year university course in business studies.

'You're a very brave girl,' Morgan said gently, 'but then I always suspected you were. Brave and honest. That's something that sets you apart from American girls. American girls are honest...but in a different kind of way. They're forthright about things that you obviously prefer to keep hidden...'

Gracie licked her lips, feeling her spine tingle in awareness of him. The room was quite silent. When they had first come in she had switched on the air-conditioning, and its soft hushing noise in the background emphasised rather than diminished the stillness.

'It's my British upbringing,' she said brightly, flexing her legs out from under her. 'Stiff upper lip and all that stuff.'

'Pins and needles?' he asked.

Gracie nodded, stamping her feet lightly on the floor to try and rid them of the tingling sensation.

'Here, let me.'

Before she could stop him he had got down on one knee and was massaging her calves with long, even movements.

'There's no need!' Gracie said with a hint of desperation in her voice. She didn't like this one bit. Every fibre in her body seemed to jump to attention and the blood rushed to her hairline. Perhaps he had no idea of what he was doing to her, of the effect that he was having on her senses, but she was acutely aware of it.

'Feeling a bit better?'

Gracie nodded, her mouth too dry to speak.

'Walk me to the door. That'll get the blood circulating again.'

He stood up and pulled her up by the hand. She wanted to act cool and collected—after all, he had done no more than massage her feet, for goodness' sake—but her senses were shrieking and she knew that her whole body was trembling very slightly.

Anyone would think that she had never been touched by a man in her life before! What was she so worked up about? Hadn't his actions been innocent in the extreme?

She knew what she was so worked up about. She walked with him to the door and stood back as he opened it.

She had half opened her mouth to tell him goodbye when his head dipped down and she felt his mouth move lightly over hers. His tongue traced the outline of her parted lips, then he straightened up and was gone.

Gracie shut the door and leaned heavily against it. She felt dizzy. Her head was swimming and her skin was burning from where he had touched her.

Of course she had had boyfriends in the past. It wasn't a case of 'sweet sixteen and never been kissed', and her reaction to Morgan's fleeting brush against her lips frightened her. She had never felt this strange, aching longing with any man ever before. When she had felt his warm mouth on hers, her breasts had hardened in arousal and her whole body felt as though it had been melting over a slow fire.

She cleared away the coffee-cups, automatically washing them and placing them on the draining-board to dry, then she went across to the window and gazed down to the street below, trying to get her thoughts into order.

There were still a lot of people around outside. Life in New York never seemed to slow down. The masses of people that surged through the streets by day retired in the evening, but only to give way to more masses of people. It was a city that seemed to feed on energy. Gracie wished that it would give some of its energy to her. She needed it. She needed energy to fight off the attraction that was growing inside her for Morgan. She told herself that his kiss had meant nothing to him, it had been a gesture of sympathy for her, after her very private outpourings.

Still, it didn't help her to sleep any more easily that night. She lay for what seemed like hours brooding over Morgan Drake, feeling very much like a silly little girl who had developed a massive crush for someone very inappropriate, like her schoolteacher.

Except, she thought, the lessons that Morgan Drake gave to women had nothing whatsoever to do with books, and she would do well to remember that.

She wondered what he would do if he ever found out how she felt about him. Not that he would, because any such feelings would immediately place him in a compromising position, and she was enjoying it over here. She liked her work. It was light-years away from what she had been doing in London, and far and away more interesting. She did not want to jeopardise her job.

Saturday dawned bright and cloudless. Gracie had planned to lie in, but she awakened early, full of frustrated energy, and in a moment of reckless abandon took the bus to Fifth Avenue and indulged in some very non-essential clothes shopping.

She bought a pair of cool cotton trousers with thin blue stripes, a lacy shirt which she would probably end up finding very little use for, and an emerald-green sundress which made her eyes look even greener than they normally did.

Jenny's mouth flew open with surprise when Gracie staggered into the hospital room, her arms full of shopping bags. They inspected the clothes together, Jenny giggling with glee and trying to convince her sister that no one would mind if she tried them on and did a spot of amateur modelling.

'No way!' Gracie said, laughing.

'Well, just as well. Rickie's going to be here in a short while and I wouldn't want him to start falling for you.'

Gracie stared at her sister. In the past their paths had never quite managed to coincide. He worked at another location of Drake Industries, and usually arrived at the hospital after she had already left.

'Still madly in love?' she asked casually, packing the clothes back into their wrappings.

'Never more so! I've told you, Gracie, he's different from the rest of the boyfriends I've had in the past. He's special. You'll see.'

'I expect I will,' Gracie said gravely. She couldn't deny that she was curious to meet him. She wondered whether he resembled Morgan at all, and hoped not, because she didn't think that the world was quite ready for two men in that particular mould.

When he did walk through the door, she looked at him with a trace of surprise because he really was quite different to look at. He had short, fair hair and a boyish, good-natured face, although there was the same strength of jaw that showed that, if he was not a hard, shrewd businessman now, then he would be one day. Little wonder that Morgan did not want to see him flush his career down the drain by doing anything hasty.

He was carrying a huge bunch of red, yellow and blue flowers and was thrilled with Jenny's squeals of delight when he had finally managed to cram them into the only vase in the room.

Gracie watched them together. After the initial polite curiosity and the usual questions as to how she was finding life in New York, Rickie devoted himself to Jenny. They touched each other compulsively, and almost without realising it. Gracie observed it all, trying to gauge the depth of their feeling for one another. She could tell that Jenny was mad about him, and she felt that it was mutual. She hoped so. She didn't think that her sister would recover easily from a broken heart.

She was reaching down for her carrier bags, persuading Rickie that she could manage them on her own back to her flat—after all, she had managed to bring them to the hospital from the shops all on her own—when he said seriously, 'My uncle has mentioned something about my being sent on a course to Paris. Has he said anything to you about it?'

They were both looking at her. Jenny chewed anxiously on her lip, as though any minute she might burst into tears.

'Wouldn't you like to see Paris?' Gracie hedged, bending over to cover the disturbed expression on her face. Morgan had obviously decided against her advice, and that didn't bother her, but what did was that she knew instinctively that he had made a mistake.

'Not for the reason that my uncle wants me over there. He wants me out of the way. He thinks that I have what he calls "developing time" to get through.'

'Perhaps you have,' Gracie said, looking at him thoughtfully. 'Perhaps you both have.'

'Gracie, we're not kids any longer. Rickie's twenty-two and I'm twenty. Mummy was seventeen when she got married and eighteen when she had you! You don't have to be old and grey to know when you're in love.'

Jenny was looking at her pleadingly, but what could she do? She could hardly promise them that everything was going to be all right. For a start she had no influence over what Morgan Drake decided to do to resolve what he saw as a potential problem. What could she say?

'My uncle devoted himself to building his empire,' Rickie said bitterly, 'and I admire him for it. I know that it means a lot to him that I carry on, but because he's achieved success by blinkering out all emotional involvement he thinks that's the only way that it can be done.'

'Well, I'm afraid it will have to be up to you to persuade him otherwise,' Gracie said gently. For a minute she had been tempted to defend Morgan, even though there was sense behind what Rickie was saying.

By the time she left, she felt that the weekend was turning out to be less than simple. Her own emotions were in turmoil, and on top of that Jenny had confronted her with her problems as though her big sister had some kind of monopoly on sorting things out.

She dimly remembered someone once telling her that time sorted all things out—maybe someone wanting to say something comforting at her parents' funeral. If that was the case, then she would have to wait and see, but she had a sinking premonition that it was not going to be as easy as that. Not nearly.

CHAPTER FOUR

THE long, sticky days continued, oozing like treacle from one week to the other. Gracie thought a lot about her sister and Rickie. She tried not to remember all the wild, reckless things Jenny had got up to in the past, because that only served to sharpen the unease she was feeling inside. There was nothing specific that worried her, because she had since seen them together twice, and on both occasions they had been light-hearted and easygoing, never mentioning the possibility that they might be forcibly separated by Morgan.

So, she thought to herself optimistically as she dressed for work, there was nothing to worry about.

She was not even certain that Morgan would live up to his threat to send Rickie to Paris for his course.

'I just mentioned it to him to see what his reaction would be,' he had told her. She had not raised the subject with him, and was surprised that he almost seemed to be defending his actions to her.

He had hovered by her desk, waiting for her response. When she'd continued typing, he had bitten out angrily, 'I realise you don't think it a good idea to try and cut short their relationship, but I'm only doing what I think is best.'

'Best for whom?' Gracie had asked, meeting his eyes. He hadn't liked that. He'd said something softly under his breath which she didn't catch, and had slammed into his office.

Since then—and that was two weeks ago—she had heard nothing further on the subject.

Gracie took one last look at her reflection in the mirror before she left her flat. The green eyes gazed back at her calmly, telling her that she was being an over-protective, silly fool. She swept outside, and for the next few minutes the energetic business of hailing a taxi occupied her mind completely.

Morgan had told her that he preferred it if she caught a cab to work, rather than a bus, or, worse, the subway.

'The company will cover the cost,' he had said in that now familiar tone of voice which assumed that the matter had been satisfactorily dealt with, and could be dropped. Gracie knew better than to protest, not that she particularly wanted to. It was much more comfortable taking a taxi to and from work, and it allowed her infinitely more flexibility. She had started working longer hours, and without a bus timetable to dictate her lifestyle had adopted the pleasurable habit of going to the wine bar with her group of friends after work.

It was eight-thirty when she got to her office and she was astonished to find that Morgan had not yet arrived. This was unusual for him. Although his leisure time was spent in the fast lane, with the Miss Jacksons of this world, he somehow also managed to work incredibly long hours. She had no idea where he got his stamina from, but wherever it was, he had been dished out more than his fair share.

Gracie eyed the huge stack of post on her desk, and began skimming through it, sifting the letters into order of priority. All the while her senses were alert to the sound of footsteps approaching, and she was almost disappointed when by ten-thirty there was still no sign of Morgan.

A day of peace, she told herself. Ever since that night when he had kissed her, Gracie had made an effort to distance herself from him. She knew he was something of a womaniser, and there was no way that she was going to allow herself to become involved with someone who could eat innocent virgins like her for breakfast, and then still have room for the more substantial sophisticates like Alex Jackson.

She could not stifle the fluttering in her stomach whenever he leaned over her to explain something, or when their eyes accidentally met, but she could do her very best to hide it, and she did.

His ego is big enough without your help, a little voice in her head pointed out, and there's also the question of your pride. You've always had that. Do you want to risk losing it now? The thought made Gracie shudder.

She was just about to go and see Frank Lewis, one of the directors on the floor below, to see whether he knew of Morgan's whereabouts, when the telephone rang and she heard Morgan's voice on the other end.

'I won't be coming in today,' he said, typically without any preliminaries. 'I've had something of an accident.'

'Accident?' Gracie repeated faintly, sinking into her swivel chair. She could feel the colour draining from her face, and her hands trembling very slightly on the receiver. 'What sort of accident?'

'Nothing serious,' Morgan drawled. 'Why? Are you worried about me?'

She heard the lazy amusement in his voice and replied crisply, 'Of course not. I'm more worried about the workload sitting on the top of your desk!' She could have kicked herself for betraying her anxiety. So much for cultivating a cool veneer. 'Shall I cancel all your appointments, or do you want me to try and refer some of them to Frank?'

'Cancel them, and come round here. I have to get the final Grammel contracts completed by the end of the day so that they can be faxed to Paris in time for a meeting tomorrow morning.' The authoritative staccato of his voice left her in no doubt that, whatever the nature of his accident, it had not dented his aggressive command in the slightest. She could feel his energy throbbing down the wire as strongly as if he were standing in front of her.

'If you tell me what to do, I'm sure I can handle it from here. I more or less know what's happening on that case...'

'Don't be stupid! Get round here at once. My address is in the black book in the top drawer of my desk.' He dropped the receiver and Gracie sighed.

She thought wistfully that Mr Collins had never slammed a phone down on her. Nor had he a vocabulary which did not seem to include the words 'please' and 'thank you'. One of these days, when she came to her senses, she would start missing little things like that.

Gracie did not need to consult the black book for Morgan's address. She knew where he lived. He must have mentioned it once in passing to her, and she had absorbed the information and stored it away in her mind. He had a flat off Fifth Avenue which he used during weekdays, and she was vaguely aware that he also owned a much larger place on Long Island where he spent the occasional weekend, and where he also entertained clients from time to time.

Such, she thought as she sat in the taxi and watched the world passing by, were the perks of the millionaire. She grinned and wondered what was happening with her own flat in London. She knew that the rent was being paid promptly. The estate agents through which it had been leased kept her fully informed of such things. However, they were hardly going to tell her if the bath was being washed regularly, or the fridge defrosted. The two accountancy students had looked harmless enough, but who could tell?

Gracie rang the doorbell, and waited for the door to be opened. She had piled all the relevant documents into one of the company briefcases, which was so heavy that she rested it on the ground while she waited. When the door was pulled open, she bent down to pick up the case, and her eyes widened as she took in the bare brown legs in front of her. Her gaze strayed upwards, and she saw with prickling alarm that Morgan was clad only in a pair of shorts and an olive-green cotton T-shirt. His left ankle was very slightly swollen.

'You're here at last,' he said irritably, stepping haltingly aside to let her enter. His black hair was uncombed and he looked as though he had just woken, although he couldn't have because she had spoken to him on the phone a good half-hour ago.

'There was a lot of traffic,' she muttered, hurrying past him into the lounge. She placed the briefcase on one of the small black coffee-tables and turned round to face him.

She wished that he were wearing anything but those damned shorts. They distracted her, compelled her to look at the long, lean limbs, and the sight of them was enough to make the ground feel very shaky underneath her feet.

'Do you want some coffee?' he asked.

Gracie nodded, focusing her attention on the briefcase, and busying herself with opening it.

'Good. So do I. The kitchen is just down the corridor on the right.'

She looked at him as he flopped on to the sofa, and eyed her from under his long lashes.

'I would do the gentlemanly thing and rush off to make you a cup, but as you can see...' He gestured to his ankle without the slightest attempt at apology. In fact, if she had had a suspicious mind, she would almost have believed that he was enjoying himself at her expense.

'How did you sprain it?' she asked, fixing her eyes resolutely on his face and doing her utmost to ignore the pounding feeling which his body was having on her senses.

'Squash,' he said succinctly. There was the slightest hint of sheepishness in his voice, and she could not resist a small smile.

'Did the wall run into you?'

'Ha, ha,' Morgan said ill-humouredly. 'It may look like nothing much, but you'd better believe that it's very painful.'

'Really?'

'Well, reasonably so. Anyway,' he continued, stretching his legs in front of him with what seemed like deliberate slowness, 'weren't you on your way to fetch us both some coffee?'

'Sure.' Gracie stood up and, as she vanished towards the kitchen, called out with a chuckle, 'Never let it be said that I don't help invalids.'

She heard what sounded very much like a snort from behind her as she let the kitchen door swing shut. She looked around at a kitchen which was very clean and contained a bewildering array of gadgets. Not many of them looked as though they had been used.

When she walked back into the lounge, carrying the two mugs of coffee, Morgan signalled for her to pull up a chair next to the sofa.

'You have no idea how sore this foot feels,' he groaned. He reached down to massage his ankle-bone with one strong, tanned hand, his long fingers rhythmically pressing against the inflamed area. Gracie felt her eyes drawn to the slow movement. She had a heady feeling that she could have sat there with her eyes glued to the spot for an indefinite length of time. The sensation was almost hypnotic.

She dragged her thoughts back to the documents lying in her briefcase.

She wished that he would just get on with the report. She didn't like the way her body was responding to him, nor for that matter the way her mind was sending very graphic images through her head, images of Morgan in bed with nothing on at all. Morgan, long, lean and enticingly naked.

'Shall we begin with the work?' she asked pointedly, handing him the documents.

'I suppose so.' Morgan took the files from her and began leafing through them leisurely. 'After all, I wouldn't like to keep you longer than necessary.'

Gracie looked at him, startled by the tone of his voice. The words were uttered half in jest, but there was an underlying petulance which she would not have expected. Why had he asked her here anyway? Surely the work could have waited one day?

Or maybe, she thought cynically to herself, that's what you would like to believe.

Before she could look away, he raised his eyes to hers and stared at her. She reddened and glanced away. Work or no work, she shouldn't be here. Alex Jackson should be here, or any one of his leggy women. They would have had no hesitation in ladling out generous lashings of sympathy and whatever else he felt he needed to feel better.

He scribbled what he wanted her to do with the documents, and when he had finished he lay back in an attitude of an invalid.

'I haven't had a day off work for as long as I can remember,' he grumbled, looking at his leg with the expression of someone whose body had betrayed him.

'It doesn't seem serious.'

Morgan frowned. 'I don't envy your sister,' he muttered, 'if this is the extent of your compassion.'

He slipped his hand underneath the neck of his robe and rubbed his collarbone. Gracie watched in fascination.

'It'll probably be as good as new by tomorrow,' she said, dragging her eyes away.

'Well, that makes me feel a lot better,' he said sarcastically. 'When did you study for your medical degree?' Gracie smiled and he snapped at her, 'Wipe that smile off your face. The very least I can expect from my secretary is some degree of sympathy. If you don't believe that this sprain is serious, then feel it.'

There was something challenging in his voice, even though he looked at her innocently enough.

'No, thanks. I believe you,' Gracie muttered hastily, thinking that there could be nothing worse for her peace of mind than to touch Morgan, to feel his skin underneath her own. She packed away the paperwork and snapped shut the briefcase. She was about to stand up when his hand flicked out and he seized her by the wrist.

'Won't you come back at lunchtime and fix me something to eat?' he asked coaxingly, absent-mindedly stroking the inside of her wrist with his thumb.

Gracie stiffened. The mere sensation of his skin against hers, innocent though the gesture was, was enough to scatter her self-control like so many leaves in a strong wind. She desperately wanted to tug her hand away, but that would immediately call attention to the effect that he was having on her, so she remained passive, her heart pounding heavily in her chest.

'Your kitchen makes me nervous,' she said with a forced laugh, 'all those brand new appliances that look as though they've only just been unwrapped.'

'Most of them have been,' Morgan said, releasing her wrist as casually as he had taken it. 'Damn women,' he muttered under his breath, 'they think that they can somehow wheedle their way into this flat by buying things for it.'

Poor fools, Gracie thought. It hardly took an expert on human nature to realise that Morgan Drake would not welcome the idea of a woman making herself too comfortable in his flat, or in any part of his private life for that matter. He liked his women transient.

Gracie did not even know whether the well-groomed Alex Jackson was still on the scene—she had not contacted him at the office after that one time, but that did not mean anything.

'Perhaps Alex can come over,' she suggested.

'Perish the thought!' Morgan looked at her with calculated charm. 'What do you think of her, anyway?'

'I can't say that I've given her much thought,' Gracie commented, wondering how they had managed to stray so wildly off the subject of work, which was the reason for her being there in the first place.

'Do you like her?'

'Does it matter whether I do or not?' Gracie asked, dodging the question.

Morgan shrugged. 'I'd just like your opinion. I listen to what you have to say. You have an annoying habit of being right. You were right when you said that it would be a stupid idea to talk to Rickie about that course in Paris, but I did it anyway.'

Gracie felt herself flush, either from embarrassment or pleasure, she was not certain which.

'I really must get back,' she said hurriedly, glancing at her watch. She did not want the conversation to become too personal, not here in his flat, and definitely not with him so provocatively half dressed. She got to her feet and snatched up the briefcase, her skin tingling as she was aware of him limping slightly behind her to the door.

The very vulnerability of his injury was making his overt masculinity all the more appealing. That, Gracie thought, is the last thing I need.

'There's no need to see me to the door,' she said. Unnecessarily, as she knew it would be, because he continued to follow her to the front door.

'You still haven't answered my question.' Morgan ignored her remark with his own particular brand of insouciance. She could feel his warm breath tickling the back of her neck, and she shook her hair in an unconscious attempt to brush it away.

'I've only met the girl once, and briefly,' she said without turning around. There was little point in trying to evade the question, because she had found out over the weeks that Morgan was the persistent type. 'I don't really think I'm qualified to make any statements about her. I can only tell you that I don't like her, and I don't dislike her.'

They had reached the door and Morgan leant across her to open it, his arm lightly brushing hers.

'That's what I like,' he drawled with a hint of amusement in his voice, 'an open mind. Well, you'll be able to close it one way or another this weekend, because you'll be meeting her at my house on Long Island.'

'*What?*' Gracie demanded, spinning round so that she was only inches away from him.

'I'm throwing a party at my house on the weekend and you're invited.'

'I can't make it,' she said quickly. 'Jenny's coming out of hospital and I want to settle her into her flat and make sure that she's all right.'

'When is she going to be leaving hospital?'

'Friday.'

'You can drive down on Saturday morning, then.'

She looked into the flint-grey eyes and could see that there was no chance of her being able to wriggle out of this one.

'I don't have a car.'

'Stop trying to find excuses. Anyone would think you were afraid of me. You can use one of the company cars, and bring that red dress. You know the one. There will be some important people there, past and potential clients. I want you to make a good impression.'

He smiled slowly and Gracie wanted to hit him because he knew that he had trapped her and there was nothing that she could do about it.

'If Alex is going to be there, I don't think there will be much need for me to make an impression.' She hated the way that she was sounding childish and bad-tempered, but the prospect of spending a weekend in Morgan's company was enough to make her groan aloud.

'She'll be decorative, but you're my secretary. I want you to disarm them with your smile, and all the while to make mental notes that might come in useful for future reference.'

'Oh, all right,' she conceded, not sure whether she ought to be flattered by what he had just said, or vaguely insulted.

'And bring your bikini. There's a pool, and in this kind of heat you'll probably find that that's where you'll want to spend most of your time.'

I seriously doubt that, Gracie thought, obediently nodding in agreement.

She was sure that her duties as secretary did not include infringements on her personal free time, but it would be foolish to argue the point. Apart from which it would be a working weekend of sorts, and against that she had little defence.

Not that any arguments she could offer would have made a great deal of difference. Morgan had spent a lifetime getting his own way, either through persuasion or through sheer ruthlessness. He had a will of iron, and once he had decided on something he would allow nothing to stand in his way.

By the time Friday rolled round, the knot of nervous tension in her stomach was as heavy as a stone. She had told Jenny that she would be picking her up from the hospital as soon as she had finished work, and it had been arranged that Rickie would look after her for the weekend, something that she had not mentioned to Morgan. She had no idea what excuse Rickie had used for getting out of the party, but if Morgan had suspected anything he had not said so to her.

In fact, over the past few weeks, a pall had fallen over any discussion of their relationship. The silence was far more unsettling than Jenny's constant chattering about it ever had been.

Gracie shoved any unwelcome thoughts to the back of her mind and smiled broadly when she saw her sister. In what must have been a first for hospital procedure, Jenny had phoned for her hairdresser to visit her a week before her discharge, and she had had her hair permed so that it now fell in a mane of curls down her back.

'For the first time ever, I'm actually looking forward to getting back to work,' she said when they stepped outside into the sun. 'I don't ever want to see the inside of a hospital again, and I certainly won't be caught behind the wheel of a car unless everything's in order.'

They chatted aimlessly on the drive back to the block of flats. Apart from the odd remark, Jenny steered the conversation away from Rickie, and Gracie did not press the point.

The two occupants of Jenny's flat had left over two weeks ago, and Gracie had cleaned it scrupulously in preparation for her sister's return. She calculated that it would remain in its pristine condition for a maximum of a day, then Jenny's innate messiness would slowly begin to encroach.

Gracie looked at her sister tenderly. It seemed incredible, but every day Jenny seemed to be a little more grown-up. She could not put her finger on it, but that didn't make the feeling any the weaker. Less than a year ago, she would have been subjected to all the complaints about how inconvenient it would be having a big sister lurking around, tidying up behind her because she still could not walk properly, watching over her every move like a mother hen.

So far—and Gracie kept her fingers crossed—Jenny had accepted the fact that they were only floors apart with uncharacteristic insouciance.

'You'll be all right here on your own tonight?' Gracie asked, as she was about to leave.

'Yep,' Jenny answered smiling, 'don't worry, I'll be fine. Besides, you're just upstairs. I can always phone you if I need anything. Not that I will.'

Gracie nodded. 'And Rickie will be here tomorrow morning, won't he?'

'Um,' Jenny agreed, looking away.

Gracie was beginning to feel nervous again. Her attention had wandered back to the drive up to Long Island, which would be nerve-racking enough, and then the prospect of the weekend at Morgan's house. She did not notice anything odd in Jenny's behaviour.

'I'll look in on you when I get back,' she said absent-mindedly, bending over to kiss the tip of her sister's nose.

As it turned out, the drive to Long Island was far more relaxing than Gracie had anticipated. Once she had acclimatised herself to driving on the right, she settled back with the window wound down, preferring the warm breeze against her face, rather than the air-conditioning.

Manhattan was invigorating, but it made a pleasant change to leave it behind, and to see the tall buildings and crowded streets gradually give way to more open areas. It was like taking a short break from an old friend.

Morgan had explained to her how to get to his house, and he had also drawn her a map, where he had noted every landmark with clinical precision.

His house was on the North Shore and Gracie almost missed it because the only indication that it was there was a pair of large wrought-iron gates which gave on to a driveway so long that it could almost be classified as an avenue.

On either side the gardens were landscaped with rhododendron and azalea plants, and a selection of ornamental shrubs. Gracie thought that it must have taken an army of gardeners many long months of toil to have achieved such a spectacular effect. It was a bright green canvas, splashed with colours so vivid as to be almost indecent. She drove slowly past, admiring the vista.

The impressive layout of the drive had given her a fair idea of what to expect by way of Morgan's house, but she was nevertheless awed by the sprawling mansion that confronted her.

It was low-slung, and dominated in the front by four large grooved columns, which the sun slipped across and turned into dazzling white. The windows were long and thin, except for one positioned directly above the large dark wooden doors, which was round and of stained glass. Nothing like being able to relax in style, she thought wryly as she approached the front door with her overnight bag in one hand.

She wondered whether an English butler would open the door, but before she could press the bell the door swung open and Morgan was standing in front of her, casually dressed in a pair of beige trousers and a black and beige checked shirt.

'Saw the car coming up the driveway,' he explained, taking her bag from her and stepping aside to let her pass. 'I thought I'd come and grab you before you changed your mind and drove away. I had enough trouble persuading you to come here in the first place.'

Gracie moved past him, her body brushing slightly against his, and looked around her.

'I didn't think country retreats were this impressive,' she said, eyeing the marble staircase and the grandeur of the dimensions. 'Where is everyone?'

'Everyone?'

Gracie looked at him sharply. 'You told me that you were having a party. By definition I thought that meant more than two people.'

Morgan laughed, and then lowered his mouth to her ear. 'Eight people,' he whispered soothingly, 'so there's no need to be nervous. And they're by the pool, having drinks. Shall I show you to your room? Then you can slip into that bikini I asked you to bring and join them.'

He slid his arm across her waist and led her up the staircase. It was an unconscious gesture, but Gracie wished that he had not done it, because she suddenly had a heady longing for his hand to drift just that little bit higher and to cup her breast. She was not wearing a bra, and she could feel her nipples aching to be caressed.

Every time he came close to her she felt this way, and every time she was furious with herself for her reaction. Was she so big a fool? Didn't she realise the folly of letting herself become emotionally seduced by this man? Especially when his girlfriend was sunning herself by the pool, for heaven's sake?

When he threw open the door to her bedroom, she pulled away and strolled across to the window, waiting while he dumped her bag on the bed.

'Where's the pool?' she asked.

'Back of the house. Down the stairs and then keep walking away from the front door; you'll get there eventually. Shall I wait for you?'

'No,' Gracie said hurriedly, 'I've got to unpack. I'll join you in about fifteen minutes.' Her eyes flicked across to where he was standing by the door, his hands thrust deep into his trouser pockets.

After he had left her, she made sure that the door was locked, then changed quickly into a deep green bikini, which had looked so delightful when she had tried it on in the little boutique, but which now seemed horribly minuscule. The top fitted snugly over her small, high breasts, and the bottom was a slip of material that exposed far more of her flat stomach and firm thighs than Gracie wanted. She threw a pale green chiffon shirt over the ensemble and went in search of the pool.

Apart from herself and Alex, there was only one other woman there, a middle-aged woman whom Gracie immediately liked. Morgan introduced her to all of them except Alex, who was in the pool swimming.

Two of the men Gracie had met briefly before, and she chatted to them, watching out of the corner of her eye the slim, tanned figure slashing through the water, her hair spreading out like a fan around her.

'Thinking about going in?' Morgan asked and Gracie's attention snapped back to his face. His was smiling, an amused, lazy smile that made her wonder whether he had noticed her covert glances at Alex.

'Only when the sun gets so hot that I can't stand it any longer.' She drifted towards one of the sun-loungers.

'You'll have to take that thing off if you want to get a tan,' his voice said from behind her.

'I know that!' Gracie snapped, unbuttoning the front of the chiffon wrap. She wished desperately that he would vanish, but he remained standing over her as she sat down, his eyes glinting as she removed the top and bundled it on the side of the lounger.

When she stretched out on her back, he stooped down beside her and said, 'You're much too pale.' He ran his finger along her arm. 'You look as though you're in need of a holiday in the sun, not as though you've spent the past two months sweltering in it.'

Gracie felt electric currents shoot through her body as he continued stroking the sensitive flesh of her arm. Stooping down, he was on eye-level with her. She hoped that he would remain looking at her face, because her nipples had hardened in arousal and were noticeably pressing against the thin fabric of the bikini.

'Thanks for the flattery,' she muttered, rolling over on her stomach and looking away from him. He laughed at that and got to his feet.

'If you're not in by the time I get back down here in my trunks, then I'm taking you in the water with me.'

Gracie squinted up into the sun, her eyes temporarily dazzled. For a fraction of a second their eyes met and she felt her heart leap into her mouth because he wasn't laughing any longer. He was looking at her with an intensity that made her throat constrict, then her eyes cleared and she watched him as he turned away and strolled towards the house.

My God, she thought, her mouth dry, he was an attractive man—more than that, he vibrated with sexuality—but she wasn't being the ultimate fool and falling in love with him, was she?

She tried to recreate the look in his eyes before he had turned around but, the harder she tried, the more elusive the impression became. In the end she told herself that she had imagined the whole thing, everything except her own stupid reaction to him.

She lay back in a prone position on her back, her eyes closed, letting the sun melt over her in one huge tidal wave of heat. She was almost on the brink of slipping into a light sleep when a woman's voice said next to her, 'I was surprised when Morgan told me that you were going to be here.' The voice implied that the surprise had been anything but pleasant.

Gracie opened her eyes and looked at Alex, who was sitting on the sun-lounger next to her, running her long fingers through her hair, and then shaking little clumps to get the water out. The blue, mascara'd eyes were staring at her coldly and assessingly, even though her lips were curled into a smile.

'Why?' Gracie asked. She smiled back, a broad, unrevealing smile, but the muscles in her mouth felt stiff from the effort.

'Well, I hate to be rude, but you are after all just a secretary, and you don't exactly blend into the surroundings here.' She spoke with a low, southern drawl.

Until now, Gracie had always found the deep south accent an attractive one, but she was rapidly changing her mind.

'I didn't come here to blend in with the surroundings,' she said politely, 'I came here in a secretarial capacity, but thank you for your very forthright observation.'

She could feel red-hot anger stirring inside her, but she had no intention of letting it show, not because Alex was dating her boss, but because to allow her anger to flare up would be to reduce herself to the same low level that Alex was operating on.

'That's quite all right, dear,' Alex said. 'I always feel that honesty is the best policy, don't you?'

'No.'

'I mean, dear,' she continued, ignoring Gracie's interruption, 'I'll be honest when I tell you that I wasn't surprised to find that you were Morgan's new secretary.

He always chooses rather—and I really don't mean to
be insulting—well, *plain* girls to work for him. Of course,
I'm not putting you on the same level as that awful
woman he had before you, who left to have her horrid
little baby. Good grief, no! At least you've got extreme
youth on your side.'

Gracie bit back the retort on her lips and counted to
ten.

'Lucky old me,' she said blandly, noticing with a
feeling of satisfaction that her lack of response was beginning to annoy Alex. Maybe she would be annoyed
enough to find somewhere else to do her tanning.

'I don't suppose you know a great deal about Morgan,
do you?' Alex asked with a tight, false smile. She began
spreading suntan lotion liberally over her body, tossing
her hair back over her shoulders so that she could smooth
the ointment on to her collarbone. Gracie wondered why
she was bothering, when she already had a gleaming tan.
She hoped that the sun would shrivel her into a prune.

'Not a great deal, no,' she agreed, looking at her
watch.

'We're very close, although we've only known each
other for a shortish while.'

Bully for you, Gracie thought, sitting up and looking
at the pool, which had begun to look magnificently
inviting. Morgan had not as yet reappeared, even though
she felt as though she had been listening to Alex for an
eternity.

'If you don't mind, I think I'll try out the water,' she
said.

Alex sat up to face her. 'I guess he hasn't told you
why he's always made a point of employing ordinary
girls to work for him?'

Gracie looked at the hard blue eyes, like two chips of
ice, and was alarmed at the dislike she saw.

'No,' she replied, hoping that her monosyllabic answer
would shut Alex up.

'It's because he had an unfortunate experience with one of his secretaries in the past. He joked about it with me, but I could tell that he was serious. Apparently the silly little thing developed a crush on him. Would you credit that?' Alex laughed, but her eyes remained fixed on Gracie's face. 'He told me that he decided after that to adopt a policy of hiring only older, preferably married women. Or very plain ones. He disapproves of inter-office relationships, you see.'

Alex lay back down on the sun-lounger, and this time the triumphant smile on her face was genuine. Gracie felt her face pale, and she stood up so suddenly that, for a few seconds, she felt the ground almost spin away from underneath her. Her words had dried up in her mouth. She turned away and stood at the edge of the pool, then, without thinking about it, she plunged in, head first, feeling the cold water race past her body. Well, she thought, Alex really had told her, hadn't she?

CHAPTER FIVE

THE sun continued to shine for the remainder of that weekend. Gracie swam and talked to the guests, ignoring Alex completely and avoiding Morgan as much as she could. She couldn't wait to get back to her flat in Manhattan. She felt as though she needed the peace and silence there to reconstruct her thoughts into some semblance of order.

Every time she remembered her conversation with Alex, the cold, condescending way in which the other woman had assessed her, she wanted the ground to open and swallow her up. How on earth could she have been so stupid? She had let herself become infatuated with Morgan Drake, ignoring all the alarm bells in her head, and her feelings must have been even more obvious than she thought, or else why would Alex have effectively warned her off?

She knew that there was nothing charitable in Alex's acid remarks, but then she would hardly have felt compelled to make them in the first place if Gracie's attraction to Morgan had not been written in bold letters all over her face.

Gracie had always stood on the sidelines, watching her sister dash from one short-lived love-affair to the next, certain that any love-affair she herself became involved in would be based on an emotion altogether steadier and more practical.

She had made up her mind from an early age that she was not the type to lose her head over any man. She was too cool, too level-headed, and had seen too many girls lose their hearts over a man from whom they should have run a mile to avoid.

She had prided herself on her control, on her ability to look a situation squarely in the face and tackle it head-on. So where was her common sense now, when she most needed it?

Even now, determined as she was to slap down any wayward feelings, she still could not glimpse Morgan at the side of the pool without her heart flipping over in her chest. When he was close to her, she could feel her nerves leap, however much she told herself that Alex had been right in one respect: he could never be attracted to someone as physically unexciting as she was. He was a powerful, sexy man who could have his pick from any number of willing women. Gracie acknowledged that because she would have been a fool not to.

Just as well that there was only one more night to go. She had planned to leave as early on Sunday morning as she could possibly manage, without appearing boorish.

She had not told Morgan this. She knew that he was expecting her to stay at least until Sunday evening, if not until Monday morning, but what could he say if she just appeared at the bottom of the stairs with her over-night bag packed, and a 'thank you I must be going' smile on her lips?

He had already offered her a lift back with him into Manhattan, informing her that he could send someone to collect the company car that she had driven over, but Gracie had declined. That was the last thing she needed, especially as Alex would also probably be making up a threesome.

Gracie dressed as slowly as she could on the Saturday evening. In addition to his house guests, Morgan had invited quite a few friends and business acquaintances over for a buffet supper. A handful of them she had met fleetingly in the course of work, but most of them would be new faces. There was a certain safety in numbers, she thought vaguely. All told there would be over forty people there, and with any luck she should be able to lose herself in the crowd. Let Alex and Morgan get up to whatever they wanted to; she would head off in the opposite direction and force herself to have a good time.

She sat in front of the large oval mirror in her bedroom, with her hair tied back from her face, and applied her make-up with the precision of an artist daubing the finest of details on his canvas, using brighter colours than she normally did. Mascara, a touch of blusher, a glimmer of brown eyeshadow over her eyes, and deep red lipstick. Then she brushed her hair until it shone in a straight sheet down to her shoulders. The constant sun had lightened it in places over the past weeks, and the blends of auburns and chestnuts made it look interesting.

Jenny had tried to persuade her to have it permed, but Gracie had decided against it. She had grown fond of the austerity of her haircut and to have it changed as dramatically as Jenny had suggested would be tantamount to having her personality changed.

She stared at her reflection and decided that she was pleased with the overall effect. Her hair looked good, her skin was an attractive golden colour. Her friends at home probably wouldn't recognise her.

She grinned to herself and stood up, wriggling into the red dress which she had bought with Morgan in London. It had been cleverly designed to highlight everything that was best in a woman's figure, fitting snugly over the hips and thighs, pinching in at the waist, and curving softly over the bust. Gracie stood back and looked at herself in the long mirror in the bathroom, as impressed with the outfit now as she had been when it had originally been purchased.

By the time she descended the staircase, and entered the huge drawing-room that opened out on to the garden, most of the guests had already arrived.

She spotted Morgan amid the mass of people milling around with drinks in their hands. He had his back to her and was talking to Alex and someone else whom

Gracie did not recognise, though she did enjoy the way his eyes lit up as he watched her approaching.

Tomorrow she would revert to her normal, thoughtful, unadventurous self, but right now she felt every inch the film star; she felt like Cinderella dressed in her magic gown and ready for the ball. Except, of course, Morgan was not Prince Charming, and theirs was anything but a fairy-tale story with a happy ending.

Relish the moment, Gracie thought. She smiled as Alex looked around and saw her, feeling a swift, uncharitable stab of delight as she noticed the tightened lips and expression of barely suppressed resentment.

'Hello, everyone,' Gracie murmured, insinuating herself into the threesome.

Morgan was about to take a sip of his drink. He lowered his hand and stared at her, the grey eyes appraising the slender lines of her body, looking at the red outfit as though he had never seen it before, when of course he had because she had modelled it for him in Harrods when they had bought it.

'What would you like, Gracie?'

He swallowed a mouthful of whisky, but his eyes remained fixed on her with such intensity that she felt the blood rush to her head and she immediately told herself that anything other than polite, maybe surprised interest in the grey eyes was purely her imagination.

'A glass of white wine, please,' she said with a polite smile. 'I don't believe we've met.' She turned away and held out her hand to the young man who was still staring at her. 'I recognise a few faces here, but I'm sure if I had met you before I wouldn't have forgotten your face.'

She meant it, too. He had an open, friendly face. His hair was fair and cut short, and the hazel eyes looked as though they could hardly wait to crinkle and smile. Gracie liked what she saw, and there was genuine warmth when she grinned back at him.

'Sorry,' Morgan said with a frown, his eyes flitting from her face to his. 'Gracie, this is Anthony Palmer.

He works for Amcan, in the marketing department. Tony, this is Grace Temple, my secretary.' He signalled across to one of the four waiters who had been employed specifically for the evening, and Gracie accepted her glass of wine from Morgan with the same bland, polite smile.

His frown turned a shade darker.

'I don't suppose you'd care to switch companies,' Tony joked. 'I think my work output would shoot up if I had you working for me.'

'No, she wouldn't,' Morgan said coldly.

Gracie looked at him in surprise. Didn't he realise that Tony had only been joking?

'Isn't it funny,' Alex said, 'what a difference the right dress makes? My dear, that's a darling little dress. So *daring*. I wouldn't have expected it from you.' She inhaled deeply on her cigarette, her eyes seductively half closed as she blew the smoke out through her nostrils.

'Isn't it darling?' Gracie agreed, eyeing Alex's outfit, and not returning the compliment. It was a black, silky affair, with so low a neckline that she wondered whether it had been put on back to front. A diamond pendant nestled in Alex's cleavage, and Gracie wondered whether it was one of Morgan's little loving tokens. Maybe Alex would keep it on when she and Morgan made love later that night. The thought was so distasteful that she turned away abruptly and focused her attention on Tony, asking him questions about his job, which he clearly loved talking about.

When Morgan and Alex moved off, she scarcely acknowledged their departure. She might be over-whelmingly aware of his presence, but she was damned if she was going to show it.

Tony hovered in her company for most of the evening. In what she considered her best secretarial manner, Gracie circulated, but whenever she looked around he was never too far away, amusing her with little stories about his work and office gossip which meant nothing personally to her, but which she found entertaining anyway.

The buffet supper, which had been taken care of by a team of caterers, was splendid. It was all cold food, and presented so superbly that it almost seemed a shame to destroy the presentation.

Gracie ate much more than she knew she ought to if she was ever going to fit into her little red dress again, and she drank enough to realise by the end of the evening that she was more than a little bit merry. In fact, her head was beginning to throb very slightly.

She wandered off from the small circle to whom she had been chatting, and strolled through the french doors into the garden. After the warmth inside, the cool night air was as soothing as if she had placed a cold compress on her forehead. There were a few people wandering about, but nearly everyone was still inside, drinking and picking from what remained of the food.

Gracie strolled through the foliage towards the pool, thinking how nice it would be if she could strip off all her clothes and dive in.

The two figures at the far end stopped her in her tracks because she recognised both of them instantly. Morgan and Alex. They were too far away for her to overhear any of their conversation, but they were talking urgently, in low voices. Probably, Gracie thought sourly, making lovers' arrangements as to which bedroom they would use when they retired upstairs after the guests had all gone.

She was about to turn away when Alex flung her arms around Morgan's neck, and the kiss was as urgent as their conversation had appeared.

The sight of the two bodies close together hurt so much that it was almost a physical pain. Gracie closed her eyes, shutting out their image, and spun round, her feet carrying her swiftly back to the house.

She slowed down as she approached the open door, knowing that her face was deathly white. The slight throbbing in her head had magnified into a stabbing pain, and her stomach felt cramped. She paused, forcing herself to breathe deeply and slowly.

So, she told herself, she had seen them in each other's arms. Had she thought that they spent their free time together playing chess and talking politics? Why on earth was she reacting like some sort of puritanical little idiot?

Tony looked at her with concern when she joined him in the drawing-room.

'What's wrong?' he asked anxiously. 'You look as though you've seen a ghost.'

What I saw was a million times worse than that, Gracie thought, saying shakily, 'Just feeling a little under the weather. That'll teach me to drink too much. Tomorrow I'll really be paying the price.'

She looked past him to the open doors, and saw Morgan stride in, with Alex following slightly in his wake. His face was expressionless, but that did not surprise Gracie. She had learnt since she had been working with him that he only ever revealed what he wanted others to know, and it would not be his style to be physically blatant with Alex in public, however attracted to her he might be.

She felt again that stab of distress and turned away quickly before he could look around and catch the expression on her face.

Most of the guests were leaving by now and Morgan walked over to the front door, seeing them out without the smallest hint that it was nearly three in the morning and he must be feeling exhausted.

Alex, Gracie noted, was nowhere to be seen, and she wondered whether she was already preparing herself for a few more hours of fun. Chanel perfume, hair perfectly groomed, body long and silky. She shut the thought out but the odd images continued to filter through, like a tap which continued to drip water even though it had been turned off.

'I guess the party's over,' Tony said ruefully. 'Can I see you again?'

'Sure you can. Provided your vision doesn't decide to suddenly go haywire.' She grinned, wondering whether he had understood her sense of humour.

'I'm being serious! What's your telephone number?'

Gracie rattled it off, and he copied it carefully into his address book, then he snapped shut the book and slipped his arm over her shoulders.

She leaned against him, because that way she could avoid looking directly at Morgan. Her body felt pliant and she assumed it must be the result of the drink. When Tony leaned to kiss her on the mouth, she let him, returning his kiss with a vigour that surprised her as much as she suspected it surprised him.

'Wow,' he said, stepping back with a grin. 'I hadn't expected fireworks when I came here this evening.'

He shook Morgan's hand, but he was still looking at Gracie when he left.

The large hallway was now deserted and suddenly very quiet after all the din of voices created by fifty people, except for the sounds of the waiters clearing things away inside the drawing-room.

Morgan was leaning against the closed door, looking at her, his face shadowy in the half-light. All of a sudden the effects of the alcohol lifted from her and Gracie felt very wide awake, and acutely aware of his masculinity.

Dammit, she thought, you're doing it again, and she turned away to go upstairs, trying to make her 'good-night' sound as bright and carefree as possible.

She almost fell back when she felt Morgan's hand close around her wrist.

'What was the meaning of that?' he said savagely. He had stepped out into the light and Gracie looked up at him, starting back when she saw the angry glint in his eyes.

'What was the meaning of what?'

He stepped closer to her, and she stepped back. She had a fleeting mental picture of them stepping their way like that up the stairs, like two dance partners performing in time to an invisible orchestra, and she giggled.

'Please,' he bit out sarcastically, 'share the joke with me. It may be late, but I'm always ready to hear something funny. Only make sure that it is funny, because I'm really in no mood to tolerate anything else.'

You're in no mood to tolerate anything else? Gracie wanted to scream. What kind of mood do you think I'm in? She tugged against the pressure he was applying to her wrist, but, instead of it making him release her, he tightened his hold.

All she wanted to do right now was to go up to her bedroom, slip out of her red dress, lie on the bed and sleep for so long that, when she awakened, this silly, obsessive infatuation with Morgan Drake would be wiped clean from her head.

'Great party,' she said unsteadily, giving up the struggle to get away from him and avoiding looking at those flint-grey eyes which were narrowed on her face and which were making her feel very uncomfortable. 'Terrific food. Do you normally get caterers to come in and do everything? I suppose it must take all the strain of party-giving away from you. I mean, I can't picture you slaving over a hot stove, knocking up hundreds of vol-au-vents and chicken puffs.' She laughed, but her laugh sounded false and eventually disintegrated into a giggle. Her head felt as though it were swimming. She assumed it was the effects of the drink washing over her again.

'Did you have to flaunt yourself in that dress?' Morgan bit out. His voice was hard and every word seemed to bounce in her head. She put her free hand to her temple and winced slightly.

'You insisted on buying it for me,' she said faintly, 'and I wasn't *flaunting* myself in it.' If you want to discuss flaunting, she thought, let's discuss Alex for a moment, let's discuss the two of you in each other's arms by the pool.

'I don't think Tony would agree with you. I thought his eyes were going to pop out when he saw you.'

'Tony was nice,' Gracie muttered stubbornly. 'I liked him.'

'That was no reason to hurl yourself at him!'

The anger in Morgan's eyes confused her. She could not even begin to try to fathom it out, though, because she was feeling dizzy and suddenly very tired.

She was not accustomed to drink—the odd glass of wine after work, maybe, but certainly nothing like the series of brandies and ports which she had been having throughout the evening. She could vaguely remember drinking two glasses of port in very quick succession after she had returned from her walk in the garden.

'You were supposed to be here in a semi-official capacity,' he continued brusquely, 'but the minute you were introduced to Tony you started leading him on. Don't you think that I noticed the way the two of you were looking at each other?' His grasp on her hand tightened involuntarily, until Gracie could almost feel the blood supply to her hand being cut off.

'You're hurting me!' she said in a high voice. Morgan looked down and released her. The palm of her hand felt as though it were being pricked by hundreds of little pins, and she massaged it gently until the uncomfortable sensation began to ease off.

She turned to head up the stairs, but Morgan swiftly stepped in front of her, barring the way up with his body.

'Are you going to explain your behaviour to me?' The grey eyes looking down at her were like two points of silver light. He was tense and tight-lipped and staring at her as though he was trying very hard not to lose his temper altogether.

'I don't have to explain anything to you,' Gracie said, choosing each word carefully, because she felt that if she didn't she would end up babbling and incoherent, 'not out of work. If I want to fling myself at a thousand men, what business is it of yours? Not that I was flinging myself at anyone, anyway.'

The little voice in her head was telling her that she sounded exactly like Jenny, defending herself after a night out on the town.

'What you do in my house is my business.'

'Point taken,' Gracie said stiffly, her face burning. 'Now, if you don't mind, I want to go to bed.'

Morgan frowned broodingly. She thought for a moment that he was going to say something else, but he didn't. He stepped aside and Gracie began making her way up the stairs.

The staircase looked interminably long, too long to attempt to climb in one go. She was tempted to sit down and just put her head in her arms but of course that was out of the question.

Why didn't Morgan just hurry on up to his bedroom or Alex's bedroom, or which damned bedroom they had decided to use—God knew there were enough of them to choose from—and leave her by herself? She didn't want him so close to her. Even though the drink was glazing over her mind and making her thoughts a little blurry, she could still feel that disturbing electric current shooting out of his body, piercing her skin with its vibrations. If she were stone-cold sober, she could at least hold her head up with some semblance of hauteur, but she sensed that if she tried that now, with the way that she was feeling, she would probably end up flat on her face.

She glanced at him out of the corner of her eye, and her foot caught the step at the wrong angle. With horror, she felt herself topple against him, and his arms immediately slid around her, catching her awkwardly underneath her breasts.

'How much have you had to drink?' he asked with a sigh, reaching with one hand to brush some hair away from her face.

He didn't wait for her to answer, but swept her from her feet in one fluid movement, and began carrying her the rest of the way.

'I'm quite all right,' Gracie protested weakly, letting her body relax against him. 'I can make it to my bedroom in one piece and on my own two legs.' She closed her eyes and slid her hand up to rest against his chest.

He was holding her as though she weighed nothing at all. Gracie felt an overwhelming urge to slip her hand under his shirt, to feel all that raw, lean hardness under her fingers, and she clenched her fist against the temptation.

When he got to her bedroom, he kicked the door open with his foot and deposited her on the ground, moving to switch on the lamp on the dressing-table. The light filled the room with a muted golden glow.

'You'll feel all right in the morning,' Morgan said softly, standing behind her. 'After you've had a few hours' sleep.'

'My head hurts.'

He sighed again, and Gracie almost expected him to say, 'What am I do to with you?' She sank down on to the bed and closed her eyes, letting her arm drape limply over the side.

'You can't go to bed in that dress,' he said, kneeling down at the side of the bed. 'I can't imagine how you even manage to breathe in it. Come on, sit up.'

Gracie opened her eyes slowly and looked at him.

Her eyes travelled over his face, taking in the firm features, the sensuous mouth, the lines that suggested an air of knowing self-assurance. The room seemed very silent, although Gracie knew that she was imagining it because somewhere, dimly, the bedside alarm clock which she had brought with her was ticking, and through the open windows came the occasional rustle of leaves outside.

'I'll change after I've had a few minutes' sleep,' she said drowsily.

'Sit up.' He eased her into a sitting position, and massed her hair together with one hand and held it clear of her zip. 'You'll never make it through the night if you're wearing this thing. God knows why we bought it in the first place.' He pulled the zip down and let her hair drop.

'Where do you keep your pyjamas?' he asked, not looking at her.

Gracie pointed to one of the drawers in the dressing-table, and Morgan fished out her nightie, a functional long jersey one, patterned with navy blue and white stripes.

'This?' he asked, holding it up.

Gracie nodded. 'What's wrong with it?'

'Isn't it the sort of thing that people in prison are given to wear?'

'It happens to be very comfortable,' she replied loftily. 'It's a darn sight more comfortable than all those lacy little things that some women wear to make believe they're sexy.' She thought that Alex probably had a trunkful of lacy négligés, wardrobes full of them, enticing little numbers that men would enjoy peeling off her. What men enjoyed peeling little blue and white striped jersey nightshirts off women? Gracie wondered in dismay, wishing that she had not argued the toss with him about her choice in nightwear. In fact, if he hadn't been here in the first place, she wouldn't be arguing the toss with him about *anything*.

'I can manage from here,' she said, when he handed her the nightshirt.

'Sure?'

'Of course I'm sure.' She sank back against the pillow to summon up her strength, but it felt so comfortable that she closed her eyes and decided to remain like that for a little while longer. Just until he left the room, she thought, though he was still looking at her and making no move to leave.

'Up you get,' he said finally, and he helped her to her feet.

Before Gracie could say anything, he had tugged her dress down, his eyes darkening in surprise when he saw that she was wearing no bra. He was breathing quickly.

'Oh, Gracie,' he muttered with a thick moan. He looked at her bared breasts, then raised his hands to them, in an almost spontaneous and uncontrollable movement, his fingers rubbing gently over her nipples, teasing them into hard arousal.

Gracie sighed with pleasure, so total and complete a pleasure that she felt as though she would drown in it. She stepped closer towards him, easing her dress off until it fell to the floor in crumpled red bundle. There were no little voices telling her to control her impulses now. They had been silenced by the glasses of port and brandy. Her body felt achingly alive under the touch of his hands.

When he moistened his fingers with his tongue and returned them to her nipples, she shuddered, raising her face to his, and feeling his mouth descend over hers.

Her lips parted, and she felt his tongue moving fiercely in her mouth, tasting her. With trembling fingers Gracie unbuttoned his shirt, delighting in the feel of his hard chest under her fingers. She wanted him with an urgency she would not have thought possible.

He was muttering under his breath, tiny groans as he bit the lobe of her ear gently with his teeth. His hands caressed her waist and stomach, slipping under the elastic of her panties until he was stroking her soft hair down below, parting her thighs, exploring every inch of her with his fingers.

Gracie arched her body against his, her taut nipples brushing against the hair on his chest.

When her hands began unfastening his belt, she heard him expel a long breath. He held both her wrists and drew away slightly from her.

'What's the matter?' she asked, bewildered.

'This shouldn't be happening, that's what the matter is,' Morgan muttered on a wrenched sigh. 'It's three-thirty in the morning, you've had too much to drink, and I'm acting like some damned schoolboy who has never set eyes on a naked woman before. Gracie, I want you to put on your nightshirt and get into bed. You probably won't remember a bit of this tomorrow morning when you wake up.'

His words washed over her like a torrent of freezing cold water. Gracie tugged away from him and snatched up her nightshirt, pulling it over her head. She had never felt so embarrassed in her whole life, and she knew that he was wrong when he said she wouldn't remember what had happened between them the next morning. She would remember, oh, yes, she would remember in graphic, humiliating detail.

'I think you ought to go,' she whispered, her eyes lowered to the ground.

Morgan nodded and walked across to the door. Gracie turned away and settled her body under the bedcovers. She didn't want to see him, she didn't want to think about what she had done.

She heard the little click of the door as it was shut, and she felt her body go limp as the tension inside her drained away.

There were a million thoughts flying around in her head, and none of them was comforting. Gracie lay back with her eyes wide open and stared up at the ceiling.

Her headache had miraculously vanished, and she almost wished that it had not, because that at least would have given her something else to think about.

How could she? She felt bitterly angry at herself for having shown him the degree to which she was attracted to him, for having let him glimpse how she felt.

If what Alex had told her had been the truth, if he had indeed dismissed one of his secretaries for having had a crush on him, then lord knew what her fate would be. Prison, the torture chamber, instant deportation back to England. Worse, she thought with a sour taste of defeat, he would probably be amused at how she had behaved, or perhaps embarrassed for her. Either prospect was too appalling to consider in any depth.

He would not take any of the blame on to his own shoulders, and why should he? She had invited his response. It was only thanks to his self-control that they had not ended up in bed together.

Gracie rolled over on her side, beating the pillow with her fists. She knew that there was no point in protesting now, that she would have to put it behind her simply because she had no choice. In the morning she would be calm and collected, as she normally was, and if he raised the subject she might even consider pretending that she couldn't remember a thing.

She switched on the bedside lamp and picked up the paperback which she had brought with her, abandoning all attempt at sleep. The words on the pages leapt up at her, but after about ten minutes she realised that they were no more than a jumble and that her brain was too busy running round in circles for her to pay any attention to what she was trying to read. She switched off the light and folded her arms behind her head, frowning in her attempt to harness her scrambled thoughts.

She had no idea how long she remained like that, images of Morgan crawling through her mind like tiny, persistent insects that had found their way to a jar of honey and were determined to stay there until they had eaten their fill.

When she next opened her eyes, the sun was streaming through the windows. She looked at the alarm clock and saw with surprise that it was after twelve. She must have slept through any hangover, because she felt wide awake and alert, with none of the stomach and head pains she had expected.

She swung her feet over the edge of the bed and sat up. The detailed, remorseless memory of what had happened the night before threatened to overwhelm her, and she busied herself with other things.

She had a long bath, not caring about the time, packed her clothes together and took a final look at herself in the mirror before she opened the door to go downstairs. She wanted to make sure that her face was composed. Last night had revealed to her the sheer, naked intensity of her emotions and the power of her attraction to Morgan.

She could cope with that, but she would make sure that he was never allowed to glimpse them again.

CHAPTER SIX

GRACIE had expected to find Morgan's house guests still around when she got downstairs, but apart from his permanent staff of three, whom he employed to look after the house and the garden, the place was empty. She strolled out into the garden, stopping off in the kitchen first to pour herself a glass of milk.

She had mentally braced herself for meeting Morgan. She had even taken the trouble to dress very carefully that morning, wearing a straight cotton skirt in a nondescript grey-blue colour and a cream blouse which she had buttoned the whole way up. Not, she thought, that he was likely to jump on her if she wore anything provocative; in the cold light of day he would no doubt find his behaviour of the night before incomprehensible, if not a little ridiculous. But in a safe outfit Gracie felt more in control of herself. She had pulled her hair away from her face and pinned it into a small bun at the back. She felt like a schoolteacher, which was fine because she would be in a better position to slap down her emotions if they started becoming a little too rebellious to handle.

Nevertheless, when she saw Morgan reclining on one of the chairs by the pool she felt her heart begin to thud heavily in her chest. She composed her features into a cool, smiling mask and approached him slowly, pulling up a chair to sit alongside, making sure that it was far enough away to avoid any accidental physical contact.

'You're up late,' he said, watching her from under his thick lashes as she settled into the chair. 'Hangover?'

Gracie kept her face averted, concentrating on the smooth, flat blue of the pool, and the antics of the dragon-flies as they swooped lazily over it.

She shrugged. 'I would have been down a little sooner, but I had a long bath. I didn't think that everyone would have left already.'

She could feel his eyes on her, staring at her, but she couldn't face looking at him. She suspected that her composed, calm façade might begin to show chinks if she allowed herself any direct eye-to-eye contact with him. She remained with her profile to him, and tilted her face towards the sun, enjoying the drugged sensation of the heat, as though she were being slowly toasted.

'Most of them had fairly long distances to travel back,' Morgan said abruptly. 'I would have headed back myself, but I didn't want to leave before I had a chance to see you.'

Gracie felt her body stiffen. She hoped that he wasn't going to try and involve her in a post-mortem over what had happened between them. Maybe he was going to tell her that, after her behaviour the night before, her services at his company were no longer required. It was an effort to breathe calmly, to stamp down the sudden panic that made her want to get up and run away.

'I apologise about last night,' she said tightly. 'I had way too much to drink, and behaved totally out of character. If I embarrassed you in front of your guests, then I'm sorry.'

The palms of her hands were perspiring lightly and she rested them on her thighs, keeping her face turned away from him and her eyes half closed to shut out the dazzling light.

How could you have been so crazy? her mind was shrieking at her. She had been swept into a vortex of passion that was novel and devastating for her, but to him it had probably been embarrassingly familiar, behaviour that he would not expect from someone who worked for him. Gracie didn't want him to say it, she didn't want to hear his condemnation because it would make her curl up and die inside.

'I wasn't talking about your behaviour at the party——' Morgan said in a flat voice.

'Yes, well,' Gracie cut in, wondering how she could even manage to get the words out when her throat felt as though it was constricting, 'I guess we all do things that we regret, especially under the influence of drink.' She laughed brightly. 'Listen to me. I sound like my sister! Believe me, I've never acted so stupidly in my life before, and I have no intention of letting it happen again.'

She could feel her pride struggling against a heady desire to throw herself into his arms, against her infatuation with him, against something even deeper that she was unwilling to explore. She knew that her pride would win, its roots were too deep for it not to.

'If you want me to, I'll hand in my resignation,' she continued in the same safe, hard voice. There, she thought, you've at least given him the option.

'Resignation? What the hell are you talking about? Is that what you want to do?'

'Of course not!' Gracie said sharply.

'I don't want your resignation. As you said,' he mocked, 'we all behave *regrettably* sometimes, especially under the influence of drink. I suppose you've discovered that it's not a pleasant experience? Next time, you'd better be a bit more careful, though; you could find yourself in a situation which is slightly more than just *unpleasant*.'

'There won't be a next time,' she retorted coldly.

'No. I'm sure there won't be. You'll make sure that you never again drop that iron-clad self-control of yours.'

It was exactly what she had been about to say, but nevertheless his frankness hurt her. His tone had been scathing, as though he had been accusing her of something far worse than self-restraint.

'I've already packed,' she said, gazing down at her fingers. 'If it's all the same to you, I think I'll start heading home now. There are a few things in the flat that I want to do when I get back, and I'd like to check on Jenny to make sure that she's all right.'

'Why shouldn't she be all right?' Morgan asked, his lips twisting. 'She has my nephew there looking after her, hasn't she?'

Gracie looked at him in surprise and their eyes met. 'I didn't think you knew,' she stammered.

'Of course I know. Rickie told me that he couldn't make it down here because he had a stag party to go to last night. The boy should know better than to lie to me. I saw through him instantly, and then I had one of my men double-check just to be absolutely certain.'

'You have no right to spy on them!' Gracie said angrily.

'Well, well, well,' he laughed, 'you'd better be careful, your mask is slipping. I can see some emotion there. Is that because we're talking about your sister, and she's the only person you care enough about to let your real feelings show?'

'No, it's because it's wrong for you to pry into other people's lives!'

She had thought she might be able to pierce through his armour, but instead of reacting angrily Morgan linked his hands behind his head and relaxed back, stretching his long legs out in front of him. Gracie followed the line of his hard thigh, and the memory of her fingers, struggling to unclasp his belt, to feel his warm naked body next to hers, jumped out at her.

'Well you can tell your sister that I've made a decision,' Morgan said neutrally. 'You can tell her that I've decided to send Rickie on the next course in Paris, which is in two weeks' time, so they might as well make the most of each other while they have the time.'

He stood up and walked away. Gracie stared at his departing back with a cold feeling. She didn't know what had made him suddenly decide on this course of action, but she felt instinctively that it had been a spur-of-the-moment decision.

For reasons best known to him, he was in a filthy temper. Perhaps it had something to do with Alex. She hadn't seen the other woman, and she had not wanted to betray interest by asking Morgan where she was, or whether she had left.

She sat by the pool for a while longer, suddenly irritated by the peaceful buzzing sounds of the dragon-flies. It seemed to echo her own irritation at herself for being so fiercely attracted to a man when cool reasoning told her that it was a mistake. He was her boss, but more than that he was a man who was not interested in any relationship beyond a purely physical one. Alex, she suspected, would not be allowed to outstay her welcome.

Still, she thought wryly, there was no point in trying to hide what she was feeling from herself. The man aroused her. He ignited things in her that had been quite happily lying dormant, and Gracie couldn't even be sure that her response was purely a sexual one.

She stood up and began thinking about the journey back to her flat, planning her route, her brain skirting round the notion that, whether she liked it or not, her involvement with Morgan was based on something more than just superficial attraction.

It was late afternoon by the time she made it back to the block of flats, and as soon as she had unpacked Gracie went to see her sister.

Jenny was looking radiant. She had tied her long hair back, but wispy blonde curls had somehow managed to stray out of the elastic band and hung round her face in flattering disarray.

'Rickie's just left,' she said, smiling, as Gracie stepped in.

The flat was neat and tidy, and Gracie looked around her in surprise. She had always thought that her sister could never surprise her, but she had been wrong. 'Shouldn't your place by now be looking like a war zone?' Gracie asked. 'Cushions everywhere, magazines strewn on the floor?'

'Rickie doesn't like mess.'

Ah, so that was it. If actions spoke louder than words, then this was final proof that Jenny was head over heels in love with Rickie. Gracie smiled slowly. 'I never liked mess either. I don't remember that ever being much of a deterrent to you.'

'You're only my sister.'

Gracie looked at her, and they giggled. In this atmosphere of easy, sisterly companionship she could almost forget the dark clouds on the horizon. She described her weekend to Jenny and succeeded in making it sound so light-hearted and enjoyable that she could almost believe that she really had had a good time.

Funny, she thought, if she listened to what she was saying, and managed to ignore the tangle of feelings inside her, she could well imagine that she was still that cool, aloof lady who always had everything under control. The ever dependable big sister who always viewed things objectively, who never allowed the waywardness of emotion to become intrusive.

'Morgan knew that Rickie spent the weekend with you,' she said, when there was a brief lull in the conversation. She had decided on the journey back that she would take Morgan at his word and tell Jenny of his decision to send Rickie to Paris. She might, she thought, be able to persuade her sister to see the practicality behind it, even though she might not be too convinced about it herself.

'How did he know?'

'A shrewd guess,' Gracie said. 'You should have known that Morgan Drake is head of that huge corporation for a reason. He has a razor-sharp mind. I wouldn't have thought that he was the sort of person to be easily fooled.'

'What did he say?'

Gracie sighed and sat back in her chair, her head tilted back slightly, her eyes half closed. 'He's going to send Rickie on that course,' she said wearily, 'in two weeks' time.' She waited for the explosion, but her statement was met with silence.

She looked at Jenny, puzzled by her calm acceptance of Morgan's intention. 'Don't be too upset,' she said, unnecessarily because her sister did not look in the least upset. 'It might do you both good to be apart for a while. If the relationship survives the separation, then that's a pretty good indication of its strength.'

Gracie watched her sister carefully, and wondered what was going through that pretty head. She had always thought that Jenny was one of those transparent people whose emotions could be read like a book. Now she wasn't too sure.

'Maybe you're right,' Jenny said after a while. She shrugged as though the question wasn't that important anyway, and began to idly trace the outlines of the flowers on her dress.

'So,' Gracie said brightly, 'you're not too disturbed by it.'

Another little shrug. 'I'm sure everything will work out for the best.'

Back in her own flat, Gracie tried to unravel what it was about her sister's placid reaction that was so unsettling. After all, Jenny had responded with level-headed maturity, and wasn't that what Gracie had hoped for? Hadn't she gone prepared to convince Jenny that a few months away from Rickie was not necessarily a bad thing?

She should, she thought, be pleased that the matter had been sorted out with so little debate. She told herself that she was pleased, and spent the remainder of the evening watching television and ironing.

Morgan was already in when Gracie arrived at work the following morning. The adjoining door between their offices was shut, but she could see him pacing up and down in front of his desk, speaking rapidly into the small dictating machine.

She was gazing absent-mindedly at the stack of work which he had left on her desk, wondering where to start, when the door between their offices was flung open. Gracie turned around reluctantly. She had a headache and she had a feeling that it was not going to get any better. She didn't need to talk to Morgan to know that he was in one of his aggressive moods, when everything had to be done in time for yesterday.

'Gracie, in here, please. Now.'

Yessir, she thought sarcastically, snatching up her pad and pencil. Morgan was gazing broodingly out of the window and didn't turn around when she entered.

'I'm ready,' Gracie prompted, looking at the broad back and feeling that familiar twinge of awareness.

'For what?' He turned around and stared at her, his grey eyes flicking over her body in quick, restless appraisal.

Gracie lowered her eyes. 'To take shorthand,' she answered patiently. He was in an odd mood and it made her wary.

'Did I say that I called you in here to take shorthand?'

'No,' she admitted, feeling hot and bothered. She was angry with herself for feeling hot and bothered, and vaguely angry with him for making her feel hot and bothered.

'I called you in here to tell you that I'm taking you out to dinner tonight.'

'What?'

'Are you deaf? I'm taking you out to dinner tonight.'

Gracie looked at him in startled surprise, then her instinct for self-protection locked into gear, and she said quietly, 'I'm afraid I can't come. I have a date.'

'Break it.'

His tall figure towered over her and she could feel her will-power beginning to float away from her. She told herself that she had spent the past few hours hardening her resolve, trying to coat her emotions with a hard outer layer of reason that could protect her from his impact.

She listened to that internal voice of logic, and said, 'All right.'

She could have kicked herself. Why had she agreed to see him out of work? Hadn't she learnt anything at all from her experiences at his house? She had seen him with Alex by the pool, locked in each other's arms. Wasn't that reason enough to steer clear of him?

'I'll pick you up at seven-thirty. Now we can start work.' He sat at his desk, with the assurance of someone who had concluded a matter to his satisfaction, and began dictating to her. Gracie transcribed his words on to her pad, her hand flying over the sheets of paper, but she was doing it automatically because her mind was miles away. Drifting in realms that had nothing whatsoever to do with work.

Did she have some sort of suicidal tendency? Her mind had issued enough warnings to her, and yet she had deliberately ignored all of them. Why did her body continually seem to act on her behalf, even when she didn't want it to, even when she wanted her head to do the responding?

Because you're crazy, she said to herself. A certifiable case, in fact.

When she heard the doorbell ring that evening she went to answer it with the knowledge that she was as much in possession of her faculties now as she would ever be.

Morgan was leaning against the door-frame, still in his work clothes, though he was no longer wearing his tie and the top two buttons of his cream silk shirt were undone. He looked at her with an expression that suggested that he could see exactly what impression she wanted to make with her placid navy blue outfit and flat white sandals.

'You look lovely,' he said with a slight smile, 'charming. Light gold with pink cheeks, like a peach.'

'Thank you,' Gracie murmured uncomfortably. She had not expected this, but then when had Morgan ever acted according to her expectations? 'Would you like to come in?'

'Not right now. The table's booked for eight-thirty, so we might as well make a move. We can have a drink before we eat.'

Gracie locked the door behind her, feeling her heartbeat quicken as Morgan linked her arm through his. She made no attempt to extricate herself because she wanted him to believe that she was totally in control. If he believed that she was, then she might start believing it herself.

He had chosen a small restaurant which had an atmosphere of expensive intimacy about it. A deferential waiter showed them to their table and took their drinks order, then faded away with such practised skill that Gracie thought he would have made a good magician.

'This is a delightful little place,' she commented, looking around her. 'Do you come here often?'

'Only occasionally.' He looked at her and there was a mocking, caressing quality in his eyes that made the blood suddenly rush to her head.

The recognition that he was dangerous hit her like a physical blow. His sex appeal was formidable. He was aware of that, accepted it as naturally as people accepted the colour of their hair or the shape of their noses.

She thought that he was going to expand on his statement, but instead he began talking about a play which he had just seen, telling her that she ought to go and see it. Now that the conversation was within safer territory, Gracie relaxed, enjoying the delicate fish steak on her plate, and lightly discussing the merits of Broadway over the London theatre.

'Do you miss England?' he asked curiously, after the waiter had cleared their plates away.

Gracie gave the matter a few seconds of serious thought. 'I don't think so,' she said slowly. 'I miss a few things, like walking through Hyde Park on a sunny day, or watching the buskers in Covent Garden, but on the whole I don't pine for it. Perhaps the novelty of living in New York still hasn't worn off.'

'And when it does?'

'I suppose I'll return to England then.' She didn't want to think of that point in the future, which she knew would come sooner or later. The thought of never seeing Morgan again made her mind go numb. It was a bridge which she would cross when she came to it and not a minute sooner. 'I told Jenny about your decision to send Rickie to Paris on that course,' she said, to divert the conversation. 'I was amazed by her reaction. No hysterics, no weeping and wailing.'

'Rickie seemed to accept it without too much fuss, as well. Should we be suspicious?'

He looked at her, and Gracie felt a warm glow spread through her body.

'There's nothing we could do, even if we were deeply suspicious,' she said. 'I mean, we can hardly keep them locked in their respective apartments forever, hoping that whatever they feel for each other will wear off.'

'No. Emotions are like that, I guess. They don't go away simply because you tell them to, or because someone else tells you that they should.' In the half-light from the candle Morgan's eyes were dark and watchful. 'The time apart will give them an opportunity to think about what they want.'

'That's what I told Jenny. She listened patiently, but I don't think she was taking very much in.'

'We sound like a couple of worried parents talking about their children,' Morgan said with a hint of amusement. Their eyes met and Gracie looked away, idly toying with the stem of her wine glass. She would have to be careful. They were drifting again. Away from safe waters into rather more turbulent and unpredictable seas.

'Except they're neither of them children,' she said lightly, 'they're both grown adults, capable of taking care of themselves, without any outside interference.'

The waiter appeared with the dessert menu, and looked personally insulted when they both declined, settling for coffee instead.

'I suppose you're obliquely referring to me?'

'No, I wasn't,' Gracie murmured truthfully, 'though now that you mention it I still think forcing them apart is not a good idea.'

'Too late now.' Morgan looked at her with a wry expression.

'Why?'

'Because I've already told Rickie that he leaves New York in a fortnight's time. I can't be seen to go back on my decision.'

Gracie eyed him drily. 'You're too proud,' she smiled.

'So are you.' His response caught her unawares and she gazed at him in astonishment. 'That's why you erect barriers around yourself, but that's a mistake. Don't you realise that barriers are the ultimate challenge to any man?'

'I haven't erected any barriers,' Gracie stammered feebly. 'I don't know what you're talking about.' The words sounded hollow, even to her own ears. She had a prickling sensation of being pinned down. She knew that the grey eyes were focused on her with unnerving relentlessness, and she didn't want to return his gaze because if she did she would be swept into a mesmeric trance, and then where would her defences be? He was unravelling her, bit by bit, and it alarmed her. It seemed that every time she dropped her guard he moved a step closer, and the closer he came, the more difficult it would be for her to walk away from him.

'More coffee, madam?' The waiter materialised with the coffee and she breathed a sigh of relief.

'We'll just have the check, thank you.' There was a trace of irritation on Morgan's face, but then he leaned forward slightly and smiled. 'We can always have more coffee at your place.'

Gracie watched in silence as he settled the bill. She could feel a growing sense of panic which intensified in the car on the way back to her flat. Morgan didn't speak at all, and that made it worse because it gave her time to dwell on the sickening feeling of nervousness in the pit of her stomach.

Of course she was over-reacting, she told herself. There was nothing threatening about Morgan. They had simply enjoyed a meal together and he had encouraged her to talk about herself because he was her boss, and bosses always felt that they ought to get to know the people who worked for them.

So what the hell was she so anxious about? There was no situation that she could not handle with a bright little smile. Didn't she have years of experience of shutting men out with bright little smiles?

He parked the car outside the block of flats and turned to her.

'Are you going to invite me in for coffee?' he asked softly.

'If you're thirsty.' She sat very still, staring out through the window at the long street, freckled with people strolling with no apparent urgency to their destinations.

'That's hardly the most welcoming invitation,' Morgan drawled with amusement. He opened his door and threw over his shoulder, 'But I'll accept.'

She could detect that wicked, teasing smile in his voice again, and she leapt out of the car, determined that this cup of coffee would be the fastest in history.

'What would Alex say about this?' she asked with a dry taste of nervousness in her mouth, as the lift doors locked them in and began whirring upwards to her floor.

'About what?'

'Dinner out with your secretary, coffee afterwards...' Gracie's voice trailed off and she wished that she had never broached the subject because, instead of bringing them back down to earth, it only managed to increase the undercurrent of tension running through her body.

The lift doors sighed open and they stepped out.

'It's a perfectly innocent situation,' Morgan murmured in a low voice, 'isn't it?' When she didn't answer, he continued briskly, 'Besides, Alex is no longer on the scene.'

Gracie stood still and looked at him, stifling her insane desire to laugh. That only makes the situation worse, she thought rationally, but she still wanted to laugh.

'Oh,' she said non-committally, bending down to open the door to her flat, making sure that she switched all the lights on as soon as she stepped inside. 'I see.'

'Do you?' Morgan prowled around the room, his hands thrust into his pockets, then he slumped on to the sofa. 'She and I parted on slightly acrimonious terms,' he said flatly, and Gracie wondered what Alex had done to antagonise him. The woman couldn't have been very astute, because it was obvious to even the most casual observer that Morgan was not a man to look kindly on anyone who annoyed him.

She was still mulling over what he had said when she emerged from the kitchen and padded across to hand him the mug of coffee. It took a few seconds to register when he patted the spot next to him on the sofa for her to sit down. Gracie stiffened, all thoughts of Alex washed away as she felt her breathing quicken in that familiar way.

She perched awkwardly next to him and sipped from her cup of coffee, not even tasting the hot liquid as she swallowed it.

'Thank you for this evening,' she said, when she couldn't bear the silence any longer. 'It was very pleasant. The food was good.'

'What about the company?'

'That was fine,' she muttered, placing her mug gently on the coffee-table in front of her. 'Though I can't imagine why you invited me in the first place.' The words came out in a rush, as though they had been uttered spontaneously, without the benefit of reflection. She looked away, abandoning all pretence of being in control.

'Because I wanted your company.'

'Why?' she asked in disbelief. 'You could have the company of any woman you wanted.'

'I didn't want just any woman. I wanted one woman in particular. You.'

His words hung in the air, suspended like tiny, lethal explosives which would go off the minute she thought about them.

Gracie stared at him helplessly. Her brain was working, but sluggishly, too sluggishly to provide her with an effective way out. Besides, did she want a way out? She could feel her body responding to his words, to the direct, mocking look in his eyes.

He trailed his finger along the side of her face.

'Has it occurred to you,' she said weakly, 'that I might not feel the same way?'

'No.'

Gracie felt dizzy, as though she were on the edge of a precipice, and if she had any sense at all she could walk away before it was too late.

He pulled her towards him, and a long shudder ran through her.

'I have never before become entangled with one of my secretaries,' he murmured into her ear, biting her earlobe gently with his teeth. 'I've always had a strict policy never to mix business with pleasure. You are my exception.'

'Alex told me about your...policies...'

'Did she, now?' Morgan said in a hard voice. 'That woman did way too much talking for her own good.'

He cradled her face between his hands, then she felt his lips moving against hers, warm and seductive, his tongue sliding into her mouth. Gracie relaxed against him, returning his kiss, fiercely delighting in his mounting passion.

When he trailed his lips over her neck, she arched back slightly, her fingers curling into his hair.

'This is no place to make love,' Morgan said thickly. 'Making love on a sofa is for sixteen-year-olds.'

He lifted her to her feet as though she weighed nothing, and carried her into the bedroom, placing her very gently on the bed.

'I want to be your lover, Gracie,' he muttered huskily. His long fingers slowly unbuttoned her blouse, and he groaned at the feel of her bare breasts, kneading them with his hands.

The words echoed in her feverish mind, and Gracie could feel sanity beginning to struggle against her weakness to succumb to him.

Do you realise what you're doing? she asked herself desperately. He licked one nipple delicately with his tongue, and then took it into his mouth, sucking hard on it with a rhythmic concentration that sent a series of shock-waves through her body.

He was caressing her inner thigh under her skirt. He raised his head and looked at her.

'Do you want me to make love to you, Gracie?' he asked in a low, jerky voice.

Gracie closed her eyes, already knowing what her answer would be. She wasn't ready for this, wasn't ready for a short-lived affair with him, however sexually fulfilling that affair might be. Her principles were part and parcel of her twenty-five years. How could she abandon them now?

She breathed deeply, aware that he was still waiting for her answer.

'I want you.' Desperately, she added silently to herself, more desperately than I have ever wanted anything before in my whole life.

'But?'

'But I can't make love with you.' Green eyes met grey in a sort of mute appeal.

'You've never made love before, have you?'

Gracie shook her head miserably.

Morgan sighed and lay back on the bed, his hands behind his head. She wished she knew what he was thinking, although she could hazard a guess. He was thinking that she was an innocent fool, and she supposed she was, compared to women like Alex.

'I didn't mean to lead you on,' she said hesitantly, and was relieved when he nodded in comprehension. Of course he understood. It wasn't too difficult. She had been violently turned on by him, as had countless more before her, no doubt. The only difference was that she had not allowed passion to overwhelm her totally.

The knowledge did not make her feel any better. She watched miserably as he swung his legs over the side of the bed and stood up.

He leaned over her, one hand on either side of her body, and kissed her on the tip of her nose.

'Believe me, Gracie, I do understand.' Then he walked towards the bedroom door, shutting it quietly behind him.

Gracie lay where she was and closed her eyes, bitterly wondering why standing on her principles had left such a sour taste in her mouth. She had wanted him with every nerve in her body. Even thinking about him now was enough to make the blood rush to her head.

She felt so unbearably helpless. She could do her utmost to clamp down on her feelings, could try to ensure that her mask, as he called it, didn't slip again, but would her efforts be enough? Would they be enough to quench the tide of desire that rose within her every time his body came near hers, even in the formal, clinical atmosphere of the office?

When his lips had hungrily moved against hers, and against her breasts, she had felt herself aching to surrender to him. It was an obsessive craving, and she knew that no amount of cold reasoning was going to make it possible for her to deny its existence. She groaned softly and rolled on to her side.

There was a reason why she had never felt this weak-kneed longing before. Admit it, she told herself: you love him.

The realisation spun in her head until she felt the prick of tears at the back of her eyes. She loved Morgan, passionately, uncontrollably, and her only saving grace was that he did not know. He knew that she wanted him, but she would never let him see that her responses went far deeper than that.

She wondered miserably why she had not sensed his threat to her peace of mind, from the very first moment that she had laid eyes on him. Even when she realised it, she had still been foolishly confident that she had enough personal weaponry to fight off any danger that he might pose.

She might just as well have waved the white flag from the outset. He had engulfed her from every possible angle; a single look from him, a few words, had been enough to make her forget all the arguments made to herself in the cold light of day.

What, she thought with angry frustration, was she going to do?

CHAPTER SEVEN

GRACIE arrived at work the following morning to find that Morgan had been called away on an urgent meeting in Paris, where he would be until the middle of the week. She read the hard, black, familiar writing and wasn't sure whether she felt relief at his unexpected absence, or disappointment.

She had spent a restless night, tossing on the pillow. Every time she found herself drifting into sleep, an image of Morgan would inconsiderately leap out at her, filling every corner of her mind, banishing any attempt at sleep.

He had managed to break through the barrier of her calm, unruffled exterior and had forced her to admit that she was attracted to him. Now she had also been forced to admit to herself that she loved him. She had no idea what she intended to do about it.

For reasons which she still could not fully comprehend, Morgan was attracted to her, but she knew with a resigned certainty that his attraction would never develop into anything deeper. He didn't even need to tell her that he did not believe in love, because the assumption was implicit in his every word and gesture, in the brevity of his love-affairs, in his intolerance of Rickie's temptation to put emotional involvement with Jenny over and above the advancement of his career.

He had told her that he understood her refusal to make love with him, and she believed him, but she wondered how long that would last when he must surely know that one look from him, one casual touch was enough to melt her bones.

The questions beat in her head, until by lunchtime she had a splitting headache. She took two aspirins and was

119

feebly trying to do justice to a ham and coleslaw roll when the telephone shrilled out.

It was Tony. She listened to his voice asking her out to dinner and accepted. It seemed foolish not to. She had no intention of allowing herself to become one of those women who spent their lives pining after an inaccessible love.

They went to a wine bar just off Times Square and this time Gracie made sure that she restricted her alcohol intake to a level which she could handle. She drank just enough to dull the sharpness of her emotional turmoil, and by the end of the evening they seemed to be laughing a good deal.

Tony was a relaxed companion. He was not infatuated with her, but he quite fancied her and his compliments were just what Gracie needed to boost her morale.

When he dropped her off at her flat she thanked him, and kissed him briefly on the mouth, blushing slightly when he looked at her quizzically.

'Your mind's on something else, or someone else,' he said ruefully. 'Either that or I'm losing that old Palmer magic that's stood me in good stead for the past twenty-seven years.'

She looked at the good-natured, boyish face and wanted to apologise.

'I am a little preoccupied at the moment,' she admitted.

'Anyone that I know?'

Gracie shook her head and laughed. 'It doesn't matter. I had a very enjoyable evening, and you're still one of the nicest guys I've met in a long time.'

'That word "nice" makes me shudder.'

They laughed, then he said to her, 'Can I call you again? Friends only relationship.'

Gracie nodded. 'Aren't they the best kind?'

Later on, as she was getting ready for bed, she wondered why she could not have been attracted to Tony. He was so straightforward and comfortable to be with, the sort of boy-next-door that mothers instantly liked because they offered no threat. Life wasn't fair, she thought. Just when you thought that you had sorted things out, had all your emotions well labelled and categorised, someone like Morgan Drake crept up from behind and made a mockery of all your efforts.

He telephoned her the following day, just as she was preparing to leave. She heard the deep timbre of his voice and could almost feel his forceful personality sweeping down the telephone line and wrapping itself around her.

'Anything happen at work that I should know about?' he asked. 'This damned meeting is going on far longer than I had expected.'

'Those files you were waiting for arrived this morning. I've photocopied all the relevant reports and sent them out to the Chicago office. Apart from that, nothing urgent.'

They were talking about work, but Gracie could still feel the tension flowing through her veins. She listened to him as he rattled off things for her to do the following day, jotting brief notes on a sheet of foolscap paper.

'I may not be back for another couple of days,' he said after a while, and she felt her heart sink.

'Fine,' she said brightly.

'There's no need for you to sound so cheerful about my absence.'

How else can I sound? Gracie thought. Crushed? 'I'm managing well over here,' she commented, ignoring any innuendo behind his remark. 'What's the weather like in Paris?'

'Fine.'

'Good. Give my love to the Eiffel Tower.'

She was beginning to feel tired from the effort of trying to sound vibrant, of talking to him in a bright, unconcerned voice, as though everything was hunky-dory, and her life wasn't in fact slowly coming apart at the seams.

There was an awkward pause down the line, then Morgan said in an accusing voice, 'I called you last night. There was no reply.'

'I wasn't in,' Gracie said, nervously flicking her tongue over her lips.

'I gathered.' His voice was short and dry. 'I didn't imagine that you deliberately left the phone ringing. Where were you? Out with Jennifer?'

'I went to a wine bar just off Times Square,' Gracie hedged. 'A nice place. Quite spacious. The walls are covered with paintings; apparently local artists pay a small commission and use it as somewhere to display their work.'

'Thank you for that piece of background information,' Morgan drawled. 'Who did you go with? Your sister?'

'No.'

There was another silence, and she could almost hear his brain clicking as he thought about her answer.

'Who, then?' he asked finally, and Gracie sighed. She hadn't honestly believed that he would abandon the subject until he had shaken out of her the name of the person she had gone with. He was too single-minded to let go of anything easily.

She had a sudden feeling that that applied to her as well. He had backed off at her apartment, possibly surprised at her refusal to sleep with him and by her admission that she had never slept with a man before. But how long would that last? Hadn't he himself told her that barriers were a challenge?

'I went with Anthony Palmer,' she said with resignation. 'I met him at that party you gave a few——'

'I remember exactly where you met him,' Morgan interrupted in an icy voice. 'There's no need to remind me.'

Gracie felt a swift stab of elation at the jealousy evident in his tone. She knew that it wasn't because he cared for her but because he wanted her, and he was not a man to want what he did not feel he could eventually get. Still, it made her ears sing. The corners of her mouth lifted in a smile and she doodled a round, grinning moon face on the foolscap paper where she had been copying down her notes.

'Make sure you get that work done that I've given you,' he commanded aggressively. 'I don't want to get back to a half-completed in-tray.'

Gracie wanted to protest that he wasn't being fair; when had she ever left work unfinished? But she could sense his mood, and to contradict anything he said right now would, she realised, be tantamount to starting a sniping verbal warfare. So she bit back the words, and said, 'Of course.'

'Good,' he snapped, and rang off. She winced slightly and replaced the receiver on its hook.

Charming, she thought. How on earth could I have fallen in love with you? The world was stuffed full of much nicer individuals, men who actually obeyed some of the more old-fashioned rituals of courtship, like not slamming phones down in a woman's ear.

Life had endowed him with too much charm, too much intelligence, too much power and an abundance of sex appeal. They had worked together to equip him with an attitude of nonchalant assurance that he would get whatever he wanted, and he did. Usually without the slightest bit of difficulty.

He disproved the idea that rich men were hunted by women who were only interested in the size of their bank accounts. Morgan, Gracie thought, was one of those men who could be penniless and still fascinate any woman to the point where attraction became obsession. She wondered whether it was the suspicion of ruthlessness behind his hard, dark good looks that contributed to his sensuality.

Whatever it was, it had worked a treat on her. He had not given her a definite date for his return to New York, and she thought with relief that a few more days in Paris would give her the breathing space which she so desperately needed.

She went to see Jenny that evening, partly to stop herself from sitting alone in the flat and brooding. Brooding was an occupation which she was becoming far too adept at for her liking.

'I was just about to come and see you,' Jenny said, when she opened the door.

'I take it you and your crutches are about to part company?' Gracie looked at her sister warmly. There was an air of nervous anticipation about her, and Gracie put it down to the fact that she was restless about the prospect of being able to function outdoors again.

'I think I'll keep them as a souvenir,' she giggled. 'I'll look at them every time I think of doing something that I shouldn't.'

'Looking forward to work next week?' Gracie asked, following her sister into the kitchen and idly scanning the spice rack as Jenny put the kettle to boil. Despite the hot weather, neither of them had managed to give up their liking for tea. It was one of their habits that always brought home to Gracie that, however much she enjoyed New York, she was still very English at heart.

'Um,' Jenny answered non-committally. 'Fancy a biscuit with your cup?'

Gracie shook her head and they went out into the living-room and sank down on to the sofa.

'I guess you're beginning to miss Rickie, even though he doesn't leave for Paris until next week?'

Jenny closed her eyes and leaned back against the deep couch. 'We won't be separated,' she said languidly, scooping her hair up from behind her and letting it hang over the back of the chair. 'We're in love. Morgan can't understand that because he's never been in love. If he ever had been, he would have realised that it's much more important than a silly old job.'

'It's not just a silly old job,' Gracie protested, secretly agreeing with what her sister was saying, but somehow feeling compelled to defend Morgan. 'Rickie's in line to take over the running of the company from Morgan. He has certain duties.'

'You're beginning to sound just like that uncle of his,' Jenny said, without opening her eyes. 'Anyone would think that you had a crush on the guy. Anyway, it's silly to discuss this, because what will happen will happen, and no amount of discussion is going to change that.'

Gracie threw a suspicious look at her sister. Jenny had changed, that was obvious enough. But essentially there were some things about her that would never change. She had always been volatile and passionate, and she always would be. So her cool attitude now was puzzling.

'You're talking in riddles,' Gracie said, trying not to betray too much curiosity. That would be the one thing to warn her sister off. 'But perhaps you're right. Talking about it *ad infinitum* won't change a thing. I just thought that it might help to get it off your chest.'

'I appreciate it,' Jenny replied airily. 'I've been cooped up for so long that I look quite pale next to you, don't I?'

Gracie frowned, but allowed the conversation to be diverted. If Jenny didn't want to be open with her, then as sure as day followed night there was no point in trying to force it. Jenny could dig her heels in quite effectively when she wanted to, and right now was one of those times.

She drank her tea, and chatted about her date with Tony, noticing with wry amusement that Jenny actually shook herself out of her languor and took a lively interest in that. When she began asking whether it was serious, Gracie laughed and decided that it was time to go.

It had been a mistake mentioning it, because it only succeeded in bringing home to her the fact that her emotions were too locked up somewhere else for her to have any left for Tony, or anyone else for that matter.

She was turning to leave, when Jenny suddenly threw her arms around her neck.

'I do love you, sis,' she said. She was quite dry-eyed, but there was the threat of tears in her voice, and Gracie looked at her in alarm. The vague unease which she had been feeling recently in Jenny's company now snaked through her.

'What is all this about?' she asked urgently. She had a feeling that it would be perfectly clear, if she looked hard enough, but her brain was too preoccupied with other things for it to function with its normal accuracy when it came to her sister.

'Nothing!'

'Nothing? You're not pregnant, are you?'

'Don't be daft! I know I do silly things, but making love to Rickie on a hospital bed, with a leg in plaster, has not been one of them!'

Gracie emitted a sigh of relief.

'Can't I give you a hug now and again without the third degree?'

Jenny was grinning, but the mulish, 'I'm fine don't press me' look was back in her eyes. Gracie wished, not for the first time, that their mother were still alive. Mothers had an uncanny insight into their daughters. All Gracie could do was accept what Jenny told her. She had enough worries in her own life at the moment to take on her sister's, especially when her sister's worries had not even been voiced. Gracie only had a hunch that there was something afoot, and, she admitted to herself, in her present, over-sensitive frame of mind her hunches might be wildly off target.

The following day the sunny weather broke, and Gracie ran to catch a taxi into work, her bag held over her head, the rain slating down from the sky as though determined to make up for the weeks of fine weather.

The short dash from the taxi to the office was enough to saturate her clothes and she dripped into the office, squeezing her hair tightly in the hands to try and drain it of some of the water.

'You should buy an umbrella.'

Gracie swung round. The last person she had expected to see was Morgan, but there he was, standing in the doorway of his office, looking at her with a trace of enjoyment.

'You're supposed to be in Paris,' she said accusingly. Her heart had speeded up and she could feel herself turning red as his eyes travelled the length of her body, taking in her wet cotton dress which clung provocatively over her body, clearly revealing the gentle swell of her breasts and the outline of her nipples underneath her bra.

'I left Stewart Hanway over there to wrap things up. He needs the experience, apart from anything else.'

He strolled over to where she was standing by her desk and perched on the edge so that his eyes were on a perfect level with her breasts. They almost ached to be touched, and Gracie sat down hurriedly.

'I have a list of telephone calls that need to be returned,' she said, fishing a message pad from her desk drawer. She didn't know how long he intended sitting where he was, but his presence was disconcerting her. If he stopped looking at her and started looking at something else, she might be able to relax a little. She handed him the list of callers and hoped that he would leave her in peace.

'Thanks,' he said, scanning the messages. He looked up and his eyes met hers. 'I have a few changes to the work that I told you to start on over the phone.' He reached for a file which was lying on the top of her tray and stepped behind her, bending over her, his hands on either side of her body. Gracie could feel his warm breath against her neck as he spoke, and she kept perfectly still, not trusting herself to move an inch.

She knew that he was perfectly aware of the electricity flowing between them and in fact was probably subtly creating the atmosphere by standing just that fraction too close to her than was strictly necessary.

It dawned on her that he was playing a game, a game of slow and patient seduction.

'Any problems?' he asked, when he had finished giving her his instructions. He stood up and she could feel his grey eyes boring into her from behind.

'I don't think so,' Gracie said, controlling the tremor in her voice. She pointedly turned towards her word processor and slipped in a disk, flicking through for the right program. After a short while, Morgan returned to his office and Gracie breathed out deeply.

How was she going to stand this? When he stood next to her, he seemed to be telling her that they wanted each other, tempting her to go to him, even though he never uttered a word to that effect.

She spent the rest of that day in nervous anticipation, one eye on her work, the other on the door to his office, her body tensing every time he was in the room with her.

By the time five o'clock rolled round she felt like a piece of tautly stretched wire on the verge of snapping. She hurriedly stacked her files together and almost ran along the soft, carpeted corridor to the lift, hardly hearing the footsteps behind her until Morgan was alongside. He threw her an oblique, mocking smile.

'You're in a rush tonight, Gracie,' he said, leaning against the wall as they waited for the lift to arrive.

Gracie looked at him, feeling herself become hypnotised by those grey eyes which seemed to have the ability to repel all her attempts at resistance. It took sheer willpower to avert her eyes.

'You ran off before I could point out a few corrections that need to be made tomorrow when you get in.'

'You could have left them on my desk.'

The lift bell pinged and the doors opened. 'Let it go,' he commanded. 'Let's go to the boardroom, and I'll quickly run through these with you.'

'Can't you do it tomorrow morning?' Gracie asked with a hint of desperation in her voice.

'I want you to do this first thing, and I may not be in until around lunchtime. I have a breakfast meeting with the people from Servane.'

She sighed and watched the lift doors shut with the sensation of just having missed a lifebelt which had been thrown in her direction. She knew that trying to avoid Morgan was not a ploy which would work for very long, but it would at least give her time to try and think of some way to fight her attraction to him.

She walked with him to the boardroom in silence, eyeing him cautiously as he closed the heavy wooden doors behind them.

He sat on the large, oblong black table, and beckoned her across with his finger. Gracie stood next to him. She had an insane impulse to reach out and touch him, and she stuck her hands determinedly into the pockets of her dress. She listened as he began to flick through what he wanted her to do, nodding at his instructions, not terribly sure why he could not simply have written the annotations in the margins of the typed document.

'All right,' she said, when he had finished talking, 'I think I've got that. Will you leave the papers on my desk, or do you want me to take them back myself?'

'Oh, I'll leave them,' Morgan said breezily. 'I wouldn't want to keep you here a moment longer than necessary.'

Gracie looked at him impatiently, 'When have I ever complained about having to do overtime?' she asked.

'You didn't have a boyfriend before.' Morgan stared at her, and he wasn't smiling now. His face was hard and serious. She should have felt at an advantage standing over him, when he was still seated on the table, but she didn't. The room was very quiet and she could feel the silence thickening around her, allowing her no distractions at all, forcing her to focus all her attention on the man whose eyes were fixed on her face.

'What are you talking about?' Gracie stammered in confusion.

'I hope you're not trying to make me jealous,' he continued harshly. 'I may have had one sleepless night last night, but I don't intend to make a habit of it, and I certainly don't appreciate women who use tactics like that.'

'I don't know what you're talking about,' Gracie replied dumbly.

'I'm talking about you and this Palmer boy,' Morgan said, enunciating every word very carefully.

Gracie's eyes widened. 'Tony?'

Morgan's gaze flicked impatiently over her, 'Of course Tony. What other Palmer boy could I be talking about? The boy you had a date with last night. You made sure that you threw that in my face, didn't you?'

There was a sullen anger about him, almost as though he realised that he was acting out of character, and resented it. He stood up and glared at her, and Gracie almost wanted to smile because for the first time since she had met him she could see that he was in the unusual position of feeling discomfort. He was jealous. She had detected it over the phone when she had spoken with him the day before, and it was more than apparent now in the rigid stamp of his features.

'Tony and I went out for a friendly meal,' she said calmly, 'if it's any of your business.'

'And?'

'And what? You have no right to probe my personal life! What I do in my private time is my own concern.'

'He's a very conventional young man, Tony,' Morgan said in a soft, musing voice. 'He probably has his marriage partner all lined up. Some young girl from Dallas, with the right impeccable background.'

'Meaning?'

'Meaning that you shouldn't be under any illusions.'

'Thanks for the word of warning,' Gracie replied casually, smiling to herself as she noticed the baffled fury on his face.

It was not in her nature to play this game of hide and seek, but why should she give Morgan the satisfaction of hearing her admit that Tony meant nothing to her?

'You can't possibly be attracted to him,' Morgan said with a rising note of anger in his voice. 'He's not your type. Much too bland. No dynamism at all. Highly unadventurous.'

'Maybe I find that appealing.'

'I know you don't.' There was an edge of certainty in his voice when he spoke and Gracie almost wished that she *had* been attracted to Tony, if only so that she could see that small smile wiped off Morgan's face. After all, she had spent more than one sleepless night thinking about him.

'You don't know anything of the sort,' Gracie replied tartly, beginning to perversely enjoy Morgan's reactions. 'You only think you do.'

'Playing the tease doesn't suit you, Gracie.'

You mean, she thought, it doesn't suit *you*.

'I'm not playing the tease.'

'Aren't you?' Morgan said harshly.

All right, she thought, you win. I am. And I think I'm enjoying it. It must be the first time in your entire life when an adoring female had not been handed to you on a plate, so to speak.

'Tony is enjoyable to be with,' she said truthfully, carefully skirting around Morgan's question. 'He's easygoing and pleasant and undemanding.'

'You make him sound like a plateful of blancmange, which, of course, is precisely what he's like.'

Gracie resisted the temptation to laugh out loud. 'I didn't realise you were that unenthusiastic about him,' she said neutrally.

'Nor did I.'

The remark seemed to surprise Morgan as much as it surprised her and he glanced away with a dull flush. 'Take those papers to the office,' he said abruptly, 'and make sure that you lock up behind you. You know where the key is. I'm heading back home. I'll see you in the morning.'

He turned away and was out of the door before she even had time to stack the corrected documents into a bundle.

This is becoming way too complicated, she thought on the slow, gluey journey back to her flat; her biggest mistake had been to be attracted to a man like Morgan in the first place. His sexuality was so blatant that it should have warned her off, should have opened her eyes immediately to the fact that he was a man who could weave a net of lazy charm over a woman until it was too late for her to even think about escape.

She had tried to avoid admitting to Morgan that Tony meant nothing to her, more for her own self-protection than to arouse his jealousy, but sooner or later he would find out that no man had the ability to make her respond the way he did, that his powerful appeal left her open and vulnerable. Would that knowledge mellow his desire into love? She thought not. She had had the impression from the start that Morgan was a man who had learned to steel himself against love and romance, and more than once she had wondered why.

True, he was a workaholic, but there was something ruthless about his cynicism. Jenny had occasionally remarked that his father had had an unfortunate experience with a woman, but when pressed had been unable to elaborate.

Anyway, whatever the reason, that did not solve her problem, could not brake her runaway emotions.

She let herself into her flat, her thoughts a thousand miles away, and immediately headed for the bathroom, filling up the bath with soapy hot water. The air-conditioning in the flat was on full, and the cold air engulfed her body pleasurably. She wondered how she had managed in London without it, but of course the summers in London were never quite so unbearably sticky as they seemed to be over here.

Perhaps, she thought, she ought to return to England, resume her untroubled life and try and forget that Morgan Drake had ever existed. Time healed everything, including a broken heart.

She lowered her body into the warm water, and mulled over the prospect of what she would do if she returned to her flat in London. She had managed to save quite a bit of money in the time that she had been in New York. Her salary was generous, and the rent charged for the company flat was nominal.

So there would be no problem over money. Gracie sighed, knowing that however much she contemplated the idea, however much she pointed out to herself all the advantages of putting Morgan behind her, she could not make the crucial decision to leave New York.

She ducked her head under the water, and thought that it was still nice to nurse the illusion that she could walk away from her emotions any time she wanted to. And maybe when she had braced herself enough she would be able to do just that. Would have to, in fact.

She stepped out of the bathtub and wrapped her bath robe loosely around her, wrapping her wet hair turban-like with the towel.

She had no plans for that evening, and that suited her just fine. Gracie had always rather enjoyed being on her own, having her time free to spend exactly how she wanted to.

She had learned in the past to cherish the moments to herself, when Jenny was out of her hair for an evening, and she still did now, even though now they did not have to be snatched, as her sister seemed to have settled down quite happily on her own.

She was about to switch on the television when she spotted the white envelope lying on the floor by the door. It must have been there when she had come home earlier on, but with her mind on other things she must have missed it. She padded across the room and stooped down, instantly recognising the handwriting on the front.

She slit it open quickly, reading the brief note with the thought that she should have expected this all along.

She had found her sister's attitude vaguely troubling for quite some time, had suspected that she had been hiding something from her. Now it was obvious.

The message was short and to the point. Rickie and Jenny had eloped.

Jenny had actually written the word 'eloped' and, reading between the lines, Gracie knew that her sister was rather chuffed at having done something which she would consider wildly exciting and romantic. There was not the slightest hint as to their whereabouts, and at the bottom Jenny had scrawled a 'sorry', as if, Gracie thought, there was very much that her sorrow was going to accomplish.

Of course Morgan would have to know. Gracie sat on the floor and stared vacantly at the piece of paper.

What Jenny had done was rash, but it was more or less a *fait accompli*. She wondered whether Morgan would see it from that point of view, and immediately knew that he would be furious. There was no way she was going to be able to convince him that this was another foible of youth.

She went across to the telephone and hesitantly lifted the receiver, dialling first his office number, and then, when there was no answer, his home number which she elicited from the operator.

She could hear the surprise in his voice when Morgan realised who was on the other end.

'What's the matter,' he demanded immediately, and Gracie drily thought that at least she would not have to bypass any pleasantries.

'Jenny and Rickie have gone,' she stated without preamble.

'Gone? Gone where?'

'I haven't got the faintest idea. I got home this evening and found a little note which had been stuck under the door informing me that they have eloped. No mention of destination, or for that matter how long they would be wherever it is they've gone to. I know there isn't much that can be done about this, but I thought you ought to know.'

There was a deadly silence, then Morgan said in a voice which gave the impression that he was about to explode, 'Not much that can be done about this? Everything can be done about this. I have a pretty fair idea of where they've got to and, by God, I'm going to find them.'

'Don't be stupid!' Gracie exclaimed impulsively. 'Leave them. They'll be back! It won't do any good at all chasing after them.'

'He disobeyed me!'

'You're not God!' she said angrily. 'You can't expect Rickie to follow all your orders without ever questioning them!'

'Don't you preach to me!' Morgan's voice came back at her, hard and razor-sharp. 'I suspect they've high-tailed it to the house where his mother used to live in the Hudson River Valley. I've been there a couple of times. It's the perfect hideaway, in the middle of nowhere. They've probably gone there for a couple of days, then God knows what they'll do after that. Dammit! That boy deserves a royal hiding!'

'And what exactly do you intend to do about it?' Gracie asked coldly. 'Drag them both back here by their hair?'

'They're too young to even think about getting married, especially when Rickie's career is in such a sensitive phase. Damn!'

Gracie was almost beginning to wish she had not mentioned anything to Morgan. She had known that he wouldn't be too impressed with his nephew's behaviour—she personally thought that they should have confronted Morgan with their arguments and sorted it out from there—but he was enraged. His orders had been flouted and that alone would have been enough to madden him.

To argue further with him on the phone would have been as effective as waving a red flag to a bull, so she said coaxingly, 'Sleep on it. Things will seem a lot less maddening in the morning.'

'That damn boy!' Morgan bellowed, and Gracie held the receiver a few inches away from her ear. 'I won't be here in the morning, and neither will you! We're going to drive up to that house and sort this whole thing out face to face! If he wanted to disobey me, the least he could have done was to do it to my face!'

He slammed the phone down and Gracie was left with the stunned impression that this was getting to be a habit.

Typical, she thought, hurriedly changing into a pair of faded jeans and a striped jersey; he decides to act irrationally, and I simply have to fall into line. He had given her no idea how long this drive was going to take, and to be on the safe side she packed an overnight bag with a few essentials and a change of clothes.

She was ready by the time she heard him bang on the door, clearly in too much of a temper to think about using the doorbell.

She pulled open the door, and was pushed slightly backwards as Morgan strode into the room.

'Ready?' he said grimly, pacing around the room like a caged animal.

Gracie nodded. 'I've packed an overnight bag. I wasn't too sure how long we were going to be, so...'

'Good. It's nearly six-thirty now, but with any luck we should make it there tonight.'

He spun around and walked out, leaving her to quickly grab her bag and follow in his wake. She had never seen him quite so furious as he was now. In his usual dealings with people he masked his anger underneath a façade of cynical coolness, his face rarely giving away anything, but right now he was making no effort to hide his fury.

They travelled down in the lift in silence, but as soon as they were inside the air-conditioned cool of his car he resumed his curt disapproval of Rickie's behaviour.

'People should have the courage to face the things they don't agree with,' he bit out at her, as the car edged its way through the Manhattan traffic, 'not run away from them. He should have discussed this with me, and not taken the easy option out.'

'I thought he had discussed it with you,' Gracie said mildly, and was subjected to a swift sidelong glare.

'I didn't realise he felt this strongly about it all. The damn course was only going to be three months' duration. Any sensible person would have waited it out.'

She wanted to retort that love didn't often follow the sensible course. Wasn't she a prime example of that? Ever since she had met Morgan she had been doing anything but following a sensible course, so she could hardly agree with what he was saying to her now.

The car filtered slowly along, Morgan drumming his fingers impatiently on the steering-wheel and scowling at the traffic, as though the slow-moving cars had deliberately congested to impede his progress.

Gracie stared out of the window at the crowded streets, half listening to Morgan's grumbling but too wrapped up in her own thoughts to contribute to the conversation. She had no idea what they would achieve, even if they did manage to find Rickie and Jenny, but she forbore to say anything along these lines to Morgan.

It was well past seven o'clock by the time they finally made it to U.S. Route Nine, out of Long Island and on the highway which ran parallel to the Hudson River.

Morgan had regained his self-contained composure, and partly in an attempt to divert him from the sensitive subject of Jenny and his nephew, but mostly because she was interested, Gracie asked him about the Hudson River and its environs. Of course she expected him to be fairly well informed on the subject—after all, he had lived there nearly all his life, certainly all of his adult life—but she was surprised at the depth of his knowledge. He even knew all about the painters who had celebrated the river, laughing when she joked that he was making it up for her benefit.

They were covering ground quickly now. Occasionally Gracie could glimpse sweeping, impressive views of the river. They chatted in bursts and in between the silence was strangely peaceful and companionable. She wondered whether he could feel that too, immediately deciding that that was wishful thinking on her part.

She thought she would do well to remember that they were not on a pleasure drive through some scenic country. Still, she relaxed back against the cool car seat, seduced by the almost painful contentment filling her.

No mention had been made of Tony, or of Morgan's barely concealed acrimonious departure from the office a few hours earlier, and Gracie had every intention of avoiding the subject.

His thoughts were elsewhere, preoccupied with a problem over which he considered he should have had some control, impervious to the fact that his ethical codes could not be imposed upon unwilling bystanders.

Gracie felt this instinctively, just as she felt that his way of defusing some of his worry was to entertain her with his conversation, engaging her with his wit and charm until she almost forgot the object of their journey.

It occurred to her that she might as well revel in her foolish happiness while it was here, because it would vanish before she could so much as think about it.

CHAPTER EIGHT

GRACIE must have dozed into a light sleep. She had not been tired, but Morgan had switched off the air-conditioning, and the sweet evening breeze must have lulled her away because when she opened her eyes she realised with a start that the car was almost at a stand-still, caught up in a turgid queue of traffic that stretched impossibly into the distance.

'You're up,' Morgan said, the grey eyes softening as he looked at her, as though he was enjoying what he saw. 'I don't know why you bothered, though. There's been an accident further up ahead, so God knows how long it's going to take us to get out of here.'

'An accident? How do you know?'

'I heard it on the radio.'

Heard it on the radio? Gracie had not even been aware of the radio's being on! She looked at Morgan's tanned, strong hands, casually resting on the steering-wheel, the sharp, frowning profile, and she felt a quiver of awareness.

'I don't think we'll make it to the house tonight after all,' he said, staring ahead at the line of cars. 'We'll have to find somewhere to spend the night. I think I'll stop at Poughkeepsie and we can try and find accommodation there.'

Gracie nodded, her brain sluggishly beginning to function.

'Hungry?'

She nodded again and rubbed her eyes. Morgan shot her a quick, amused glance.

'Are you normally so silent after you've just woken up?' he drawled, continuing lazily when she didn't reply, 'Perhaps I ought to get into the habit of waking up next to you, so that I can relish the experience a bit more often.'

Gracie looked at him sharply, but he was smiling and staring ahead, an unreadable expression on his face. She had not realised before how intimate a car could be, how close their bodies were. His words were uttered nonchalantly enough but they nevertheless managed to change the atmosphere subtly. She could feel her pulses begin to race and was bemused that he could have this reaction on her when he wasn't even looking at her, when he wasn't even concentrating on what he was saying.

'We wouldn't be here in the first place if it weren't for your crazy ideas,' she said irritably.

She thought that she could antagonise him back into the present, but he merely laughed.

'I'm quite enjoying myself,' he murmured, darting another quick glance at her flushed face. 'I don't often get the opportunity of taking a scenic if somewhat slow-moving drive with a beautiful, charming woman.'

'Hah!' Gracie snorted, turning away to hide her confusion. How could she feel so relaxed with a man, only to find that a few throwaway sentences from him could have her head reeling in a way that made her feel as though she was losing all touch with common sense?

He laughed again, but the traffic was beginning to pick up, and his attention refocused on the road, manoeuvring the car into top gear as they drove past the cause of the hold-up, a lorry which had jack-knifed across the road, and which was now sprawled inert on the hard shoulder, like some great lumbering beast temporarily stunned.

The sun had dipped down into the sky, and Gracie could feel the night creeping slowly upon them. She wound up her window and tried to concentrate on the practical issues at hand: her hunger; what she would say to Jenny when she saw her. Anything to distract her from Morgan's lean body next to her.

It was dark by the time they pulled into Poughkeepsie, stopping off at a drive-in burger house, where Morgan bought two cheeseburgers and Cokes. Gracie hungrily bit into hers, not realising how hungry she had been until the food settled comfortably in her stomach.

'Does this remind you of your teenage years?' Morgan asked idly.

'There were absolutely no drive-in burger bars in London,' Gracie said, licking her fingers. 'In fact, I've never been to a drive-in anything in my life before.'

'You've missed out on one of life's more pleasurable experiences, then.' Morgan was looking at her. She could see the glint of his grey eyes and felt another quiver of alarm. 'In fact, I had forgotten quite how pleasurable this particular experience was until now.'

'Don't tell me you haven't done this with any of your girlfriends,' Gracie mocked. She didn't like the way he was looking at her, with that sexy, self-assured half-smile. It made her heart thud too heavily in her chest, made her too aware of her own vulnerability.

He started up the car, the engine throbbing into life, and began to reverse out.

'The women I usually date would be deeply disappointed if they ever had to share a meal with me in a place like this,' he said in a matter-of-fact tone of voice. 'They expect to be wined and dined in the most expensive restaurants, places where they can wear their furs and be noticed.'

Gracie knew that he was simply being truthful, but nevertheless it hurt because it brought home to her how vastly different their worlds were. The life of high glamour was not for her. She could be perfectly content to take a walk in the woods, and then have a burger afterwards. She did not possess any fur coats to be noticed in, and she certainly did not want any.

So there, she told herself, still feeling disgruntled. The car stopped outside a small hotel, brightly lit and offering twelve-ounce steaks in their restaurant. Morgan turned to her and said, 'I'll just check to see if there are any vacancies.'

He swung himself smoothly out of the car and Gracie followed his body hungrily, as he disappeared between the opened glass doors. She was beginning to lose track of why they had come on this trip in the first place, and had to keep reminding herself that the confrontation at the end of it was not going to be pleasant. Jenny could become quite shrill when threatened. All that recently gained maturity might well just crumble under pressure, like a bauble smashing on to the ground.

She watched as Morgan came out of the hotel, her eyes taking in the lithe stride, the well-proportioned body. Sitting in the darkness of the car, she knew that he would not be able to see the physical need in her eyes, and it was almost shamefully enjoyable to be able to watch him openly.

He tapped on her window and she wound it down.

'We're in luck,' he said, bending down to talk to her. 'Just. Apparently the place is flooded with tourists doing the usual picturesque Hudson River tour. I should think that quite a few of those people who were stuck in the jam with us detoured here as well for the night. So grab your bag.'

'What about you?' Gracie asked. 'Didn't you bring anything?'

'Well, I hardly expected to be holed up here for the night. I had planned on our being in the house by now.'

He pulled open the door for her and Gracie stepped out, grateful to stretch her legs. His car was luxuriously comfortable, but she still felt stiff after the hours spent in it. She let him take her overnight bag from her and they went to the reception desk.

The small hotel certainly seemed to be doing well. There were quite a few people milling around in the compact reception area, some families, most of them pink and healthy-looking. Gracie looked at one particular boy, no more than five years old, who was jumping round his sister in an attempt to pull her long pigtail, ignoring the half-hearted attempts of his parents to make him sit down while they perused a guide-book. She felt a little bit sorry for his parents, if he was as energetic as this in a car.

'We're on the second floor,' Morgan whispered into her ear, making her jump. 'We might as well walk up. I don't think your overnight bag will be too much of a strain.' He guided her by her elbow towards the stairs, his cool fingers sending little shivers through her arm.

When he opened the bedroom door for her Gracie stepped inside and stretched out her hand for her bag. Instead of handing it to her, Morgan stepped inside, shutting the door behind him and slinging the bag on to the bed.

'Not bad,' he said, looking around the room with his hands in his pockets. 'Clean, fairly large, no objectionable prints on the wall.' He lazily walked across to the window and peered outside. 'And the view is all right, provided you don't want a scenery of wide open fields and leafy lanes.'

Gracie remained standing where she was, her hands on her hips. What was he still doing in her bedroom? She didn't care for the way he was standing at the window, with apparently no thought in his head about leaving.

'Are you on the hotel payroll, by any chance?' she quipped lightly, determined to maintain her careful, composed veneer and not give him the opportunity to show her the amused, mocking side of his personality which would be guaranteed to addle her.

He turned to look at her, relaxing on the window-ledge.

'Which room are you in?' Gracie asked nervously. 'I wouldn't mind having a shower, so perhaps...' Her voice trailed off and she waited for him to read the message behind her words, but he made no attempt to move.

Gracie felt a sudden spurt of anger. What did she have to say to make the man go to his own room?

'I am in my own room,' Morgan said blandly.

'Where is my room, then?' Gracie asked, with the sinking feeling of someone who suspected that they might be playing a game of poker with a fixed deck of cards.

'We're sharing this room,' Morgan stated bluntly, 'and before you decide to have a fit of hysterics I'll just tell you that there was no choice. It was share a room, or spend the rest of the night on the road. The receptionist said that the hotels around here are all packed to overflowing. Something about the fine weather and a weekend fair being held nearby.'

Gracie didn't say a word. She couldn't, because her tongue felt as though it were glued to the roof of her mouth. How on earth could she spend a night in the same bedroom as Morgan? She couldn't. It was unthinkable. Her nerves felt frayed enough without having to cope with this.

He continued to hold her with his eyes. Gracie suddenly felt very tired. She went across to the bed and sat down.

'There isn't even a sofa that you could sleep on,' she muttered numbly.

'Why do you assume that I would be the one to sleep on it, even it there were one? Haven't you heard of Women's Lib?'

'Very funny,' she snapped. 'You might find this amusing, but I don't. I wouldn't be here at all if it weren't for you!'

'I know. You've already made that clear, but the fact is that we're here now, and we're just going to have to make the best of it. Do you want to shower first?'

Gracie didn't answer. She snatched up her overnight bag and strode towards the bathroom, relieved to find that there was a lock on the door. She wouldn't put it past him to capitalise on their situation. She wondered briefly how she would react if he made a pass at her, and felt her body begin to burn.

'I take it that means yes?' he called after her as she slammed the bathroom door behind her.

Why did everything always seem to conspire against her fragile instinct for self-preservation? Damn Jenny, she thought, knowing that her sister had nothing whatsoever to do with her precarious hold on her self-control.

She took her time under the shower, only switching it off when she heard Morgan knocking on the bathroom door.

'Any chance of your reappearing?' he asked loudly, with what sounded suspiciously like amusement in his voice.

Any chance of you disappearing? she thought sourly to herself. She looked at herself in the mirror, devoid of make-up, looking all of nineteen and transparently inexperienced.

When she finally emerged, he grinned at her, his eyes assessing her slim body, scantily covered in her striped cotton jersey nightshirt which she had brought to sleep in.

'Still believe in the gaolbird look, I see,' Morgan drawled, his words bringing a flush to her cheeks as she remembered the last time he had seen her in her nightshirt. The memory of his hands on her bare body leapt into her mind and she looked away, as though if she stared at him he might be able to see exactly what was running through her mind.

He went into the bathroom, shutting the door behind him, and Gracie slipped under the covers, forming a cocoon of bedclothes around her body, too tense to drift into any sort of sleep while she waited for him to emerge. He was singing, a full-bodied, off-key song which she could just discern over the noise of the water.

He certainly didn't lose his cool over a minor unforeseen incident such as this, she thought ill-humouredly. When she heard the bathroom door open she closed her eyes and tried to breathe in a deep, even manner.

'Sleeping?' he asked without preamble. The bed sank under the weight of his body as he joined her. Gracie held her breath, her body like board under the blankets. She knew that he was facing her and she pulled away slightly.

'No need for nerves,' Morgan drawled huskily. 'I may not be one of the world's greatest romantics, but I do have a few principles in life. One of them is never to force myself on a woman, so there's no need for you to lie there cringing.'

'What time should we think about setting off tomorrow?' she asked with as much coolness as she could muster, abandoning the pretence of being asleep.

'Wake up whenever you like. There's no desperate rush to leave early.'

'I doubt I'll be able to sleep with you in the bed,' Gracie muttered, still facing away from him. 'I'm not accustomed to sharing a bed with anyone.' She could have kicked herself for sounding so guileless.

'Pretend I'm your sister.'

Very likely, Gracie thought to herself. Easier to kid myself that you're a little green man from Mars.

There was silence, then she heard his low, rhythmic breathing. Asleep already? He must have an untroubled conscience.

She continued to lie with her back to him until she could feel pins and needles begin to jab into her arm. Very slowly she turned over until she was facing him. Her eyes had adjusted to the darkness in the room, and she looked at him from under her lashes, drinking in the sharp, clever features of his face. Even in sleep his sensual mouth seemed to have an uncompromising, incisive set to it which made her smile.

There was something liberating about being in the same bed as him, feeling the warmth radiating out from his body in soporific waves. She couldn't imagine how

Alex must have felt when he'd told her that their relationship was finished. From the little Gracie had seen, the other woman had nurtured a possessive streak towards Morgan. Perhaps she had felt that, with all her beauty and social *savoir-faire*, she might have been able to capture him, like a hunter setting a clever trap for a particularly elusive jungle animal.

Gracie admitted that she had fallen head over heels in love with him, but at least she was smart enough to realise that she could never hope to trap him. Perhaps when she left New York, clutching her unfulfilled love, her disillusion would not be quite so intense.

The thought of leaving New York, the inevitable departure, was enough to make her ache. It was difficult enough leaving the office on a Friday, to face the whole weekend thinking about him, but the prospect of never seeing him again was enough to fill her with anticipated pain.

She was still watching him when his eyes flew open suddenly, and all the air seemed to leave her lungs.

'I thought you were asleep,' Gracie stammered, because she could not think of anything else to say.

'You think it's easy for me to just lie down and fall asleep when I'm in the same bed as you?' Morgan propped himself up on his elbow and stared at her. The bedclothes had slipped down to his waist and Gracie saw that he was half naked. She knew that she must be imagining it, but she felt that she could make out every muscle in his arm. He was in a rest position, but even so she could sense the power in his body.

The thought that he might have known for what length of time she had lain there, watching him, was enough to send the blood rushing to her head.

'You're not wearing a shirt,' Gracie said unnecessarily, aware that she probably sounded as though she was babbling.

Morgan laughed softly. 'Don't forget that I didn't come prepared for an overnight stay in a hotel. I'm not only shirtless either.'

Gracie's eyes widened and she could feel her breathing become quicker. He was not touching her. He didn't have to, because the mere fact of his naked body in the bed next to her was enough to make her pulses race.

She knew what she was going to do even before she had made a conscious decision. What was the point denying her feelings, denying the hunger she felt every time she looked at him? She loved him, and if he could not return her love, then that was simply a fact of life to which she would have to resign herself.

All she wanted to do was to give up. To give up and to give in to something which was just too powerful to resist.

She raised one hand and caressed the side of his face, feeling his body tense as flesh met flesh.

'Gracie,' he said with a small moan, 'do you know what you're doing?'

She ran her hand smoothly over his shoulder and along his arm, delighting in a sense of power as she felt his body shudder slightly under her touch.

'I want you, Morgan Drake,' she said shakily. 'I want to make love to you. I can't fight it any longer.'

She felt her mind begin to cloud over as his hand curved around the nape of her neck and his head descended.

His mouth covered hers, his lips crushing hers fiercely, then trailing molten kisses on her face and neck, his teeth nipping against her throat.

Gracie groaned as he shifted against her. Her clothes seemed like an infuriating barrier between them and she pulled her nightshirt over her head, tossing it and her underwear on to the ground. He pulled her towards him, her breasts pushing against his chest. He was hard and hot against her. He muttered against her mouth, 'Gracie,

I've never wanted any woman as much as I've wanted you,' and she replied in a trembling voice,

'Make love to me.'

When he lowered his dark head to her breasts, his tongue flicking across her nipples, sending darts of intense pleasure through her body, Gracie curled her fingers into his hair and arched back.

She felt as though she had been waiting a lifetime for this. Maybe she had been. It was just an ironic twist of fate that the man who could arouse her emotions and her senses with such savagery was also a man who could not return her love.

It was a bitter pill to swallow, but she no longer cared, and her lack of caring made her movements all the more desperate and urgent. He continued to caress her breasts with his hands, kissing the flat plane of her stomach.

When his body covered hers, she gave a hoarse groan of pleasure. She knew that he was whispering to her, short disjointed words that she didn't even really hear because she was trembling so much that she felt dizzy.

'I'll be very gentle,' he murmured before he slid into her. She tensed, but only fractionally, then her mounting passion took over as his movements became strong and rhythmic. Every worry she had ever had flew out of her mind. There was no past or future, only now.

A groan of pleasure escaped her lips, and her body responded to his with a rhythm which she did not know she possessed, moving feverishly against his until waves of satisfaction flooded through her, leaving her limp and coated in an invisible film of perspiration.

She felt his body relax, though his hands continued to stroke her, his lips exploring her half-opened mouth lazily and sensually, sending renewed shivers of delight through her.

As he moved against her once more, the slow spiral of pleasure swiftly coursed through her and she wrapped her legs around his hard thighs, her body hot with passionate need.

In all her thirsting and uncontrolled imaginings she had not thought she could feel so possessed by the naked passion snaking now through her. Its fierceness left her helpless.

Reason settled back on to her when they lay on the bed afterwards. Morgan had propped himself up so that he was looking down at her, stroking away the strands of fine brown hair from her face.

'Why did you change your mind about making love to me?' he asked.

Gracie shrugged. Because I love you, she wanted to say, so how could I not make love to you? Instead she smiled and murmured, 'Why not? We were both attracted to each other—that seemed a pretty good reason.'

He gently bit her earlobe with his teeth, his hand moving down to cup her breast.

She felt her body begin to stir once again in response to him, and he must have felt it too because he laughed softly and turned her to face him.

'I had hoped you would,' he murmured, rolling his thumb over her erect nipple. 'I wouldn't have touched you, you had to come to me, but I think I would have gone crazy if we'd continued working together and I couldn't know that you belonged to me.'

Possession. Wasn't that what it was all about? The strange thing was that she wanted him to feel possessive about her, even though she knew that his idea of possession didn't stretch beyond the realms of desire.

'I don't belong to you,' Gracie lied. 'No more than you belong to me.'

'How much is that?' Morgan asked. He stroked her thigh lightly with his fingers and Gracie fell back against the bed, her breath coming quickly and excitedly. She half closed her eyes. 'You have the power to make me laugh, and make me angry,' he continued in the same low voice, 'so doesn't that give you a certain hold over me?' His fingers were exploring her body, every touch sending currents of need coursing through her.

She wanted to ask him whether that made her unique, but she didn't know whether she would like his answer. Surely other women had had the same so-called hold over him? The question of love simply did not arise. Not with her, or with anyone else, for that matter. Mutual enjoyment, yes. But not love, not that aching, powerful emotion that she felt every time she sensed his presence, every time she thought of him. Someone should have warned her that love was painful.

She ran her hands over his body, delighting in the firm, hard feel of his contours. Under her passion, she could feel the sharp blade of sadness, as though she was already thinking ahead to the day when he would no longer be around.

Morgan was breathing thickly. 'I need you, Gracie. I need you now.'

She felt him thrust into her, but this time their love-making was more tender, his movements urging her on to little pinnacles of pleasure, then relaxing until finally she had to move her own supple body quickly against his, so that her aching need could be quenched.

When Gracie at last fell asleep that night, she slept deeply, but all the while subconsciously aware of Morgan's warm body next to her, his arm flung heavily over her.

She awakened the following morning to hear the sounds of Morgan in the bathroom, having a shower. He had left the bathroom door open and Gracie tentatively got out of bed, halting when she discerned his naked body behind the shower curtain.

Her heart flipped over. He had insinuated himself under her skin, vibrated in every pore of her being.

She walked towards the shower, hesitantly pulling back the curtain, blushing as she took in his wet, perfectly proportioned body.

'Join me,' he invited, smiling. 'The water's exactly the right temperature.'

She knew that she was being a crazy fool, but she couldn't help herself. Her body had long ago rebelled against the commands of her brain. She stepped under the fine needles of warm water, arching to meet Morgan's demanding mouth with parted lips.

'My little wanton,' he breathed tenderly. Under the water, Gracie could almost feel herself beginning to melt as desire rippled through her body.

If she wasn't careful, she thought, she would be drained away into the plughole with the warm water on the tiled bath floor.

She felt almost reluctant to leave the hotel room and step outside into the hot sunshine. It was easier to forget about reality in the confines of those four walls.

'How long will it take us to reach the house?' she asked, once they were outside.

Morgan did not look at her. 'I've changed my mind,' he said roughly, opening the car door for her and slinging her bag into the back seat.

'Changed your mind?'

'That's right.'

Gracie frowned, puzzled at his decision, and by the dull flush on his face.

'Why?'

She slid into the car and looked at him. He leaned his arm along the car seat, inclining forward to kiss her on her mouth, slowly and thoroughly. 'Because,' he said in a husky voice, 'you were absolutely right in everything you said. They're not kids any longer, and if they're making a mistake then they have to learn from it.' He kissed her again, his tongue tracing the outline of her lips, then exploring the sweet moistness of her mouth. 'So we're going to head back to Manhattan and spend the day in bed.'

'Doing what?' Gracie asked innocently, one eyebrow raised.

'Don't tempt me. I might just find the nearest quiet spot off Highway Nine, and indulge in that other teenage pleasure of making love in the back seat of a car.'

Gracie closed her eyes and sighed contentedly. She didn't want to think about the consequences of her actions. There was no room for pride in what she was feeling, but there was an awful lot of room for hurt, and her mind pushed the thought of it away from her.

She watched the scenery rushing past her, as they sped back towards New York. There was a beguiling familiarity in their conversation, as though they had known each other a lifetime. Whenever the car slowed down, Morgan slipped his hand under her dress, resting his hand casually on her thigh, lightly stroking the sensitive skin.

It was nearly midday by the time they made it back to Manhattan, and instead of driving directly to her flat Morgan pulled up in front of the New York Hilton, an impressive building covered with steel and glass panels.

'Why are we here?' Gracie asked, staring up at the feat of modern architecture.

'I did tell you that we were going to spend the day in bed,' Morgan answered with a smile.

'I thought that meant we would go back to my flat.'

'And have to go out for something to eat? No, I want to spend a totally decadent day just lying next to you. When we feel hungry, we can order from room service.'

Gracie had never stayed in an expensive hotel before. She insisted on cleanliness and comfort, but with one careful eye on her finances; she certainly would never have been able to afford anything like the grandeur of the Hilton.

There was no point in pretending to be sophisticated. She looked around the huge lobby, which was as modern and clean-cut as the architectural lines, frankly impressed.

Their bedroom was spectacular. This certainly was a taste of the high life, she thought, although she suspected that a diet of this would become too rich for her in the end. Morgan approached her from behind, folding his arms around her, his mouth warm against her neck.

'Aren't you going to congratulate me?' he asked, turning her around to face him.

'For what?'

'For making it here without having to stop halfway through the journey to make love to you?'

There was a lazy, sensual glint in his eye and Gracie smiled. She laced her fingers through his and tiptoed to kiss him lightly on the mouth and the tip of his nose.

More than anything else she wished that she could feel the same uncluttered attraction to him as he felt to her. He talked a lot about making love, but she acknowledged that what he meant was having sex. In time she would perhaps resign herself to that, at least the feel of his body would satisfy some of the painful love she felt for him.

He bent and returned her kiss, lightly brushing his lips over her mouth, then the tip of her nose, finally her mouth again, this time with less restraint.

'You're quite something, Miss Grace Temple,' he said, lifting her off her feet and placing her gently on the bed. 'Don't those stiff-upper-lip men in England know what they're missing out on? All that fire seething underneath your cool exterior? I'm amazed you've never had serious relationship before.'

'You haven't,' Gracie pointed out, each word knifing into her.

'True,' Morgan admitted. 'Though I've never looked at it in that light before.'

He unhurriedly removed her clothes, then commanded her to do the same to him. Gracie didn't rush either. She liked the feeling of growing excitement that she could sense within him, as each button on his shirt was carefully undone.

'You're dangerous,' he muttered, pulling her on top of him before she could ask him what he meant.

She found it ironic that he used that adjective in connection with her, because it was precisely the word she would have chosen to describe him. She dipped her head and kissed him, her hair forming a curtain around their faces.

He'll hurt me, she thought. But right now she had no time for tomorrow.

CHAPTER NINE

GRACIE was getting ready for work on Monday morning when the telephone rang. She rushed to answer it, immediately thinking that it must be Morgan, although she couldn't imagine why he would be calling her so early in the morning.

The weekend had a dreamlike quality about it. True to his word, they had spent the whole of Friday in the hotel, only emerging at nine in the evening for something to eat.

Gracie blushed at the memory of their lovemaking, at the abandoned manner with which she had yielded to Morgan, allowing him to lead her down a path of sensual delight which she would not have thought possible.

Her love had opened her up to his every caress, like a tiny bud blossoming under coaxing sunshine. Her responsiveness, she knew, had made her irresistible to him. Now, in the cold light of day, she wondered whether he was the same with all those other women that he had slept with. She had been taught the fine details of lovemaking by an expert, and experts gained their experience from somewhere.

In a moment of passion, he had groaned huskily that he had never felt so fulfilled with any woman. A part of her desperately wanted to read every favourable nuance behind his words, but she refused to become the archetypal fool who buried her head in the sand and only saw what she wanted to see.

Oh, no, she thought, she was no fool. She loved him, but she was realistic enough to know that, to him, she was no more than a passing fancy, a toy whose batteries would inevitably wind down, and when they did she would be dropped, just as casually as Alex had been dropped. Why pretend otherwise?

Their attitudes, she reflected, were poles apart. What brought them together was their mutual need to touch one another. Her mind flashed back to the exquisite, trembling excitement that had filled her every time she had felt Morgan's hard, demanding body under her fingers, the way his grey eyes had darkened with desire.

There was no room for regrets, even though she suspected that her life would have been considerably easier if she had been able to control her own desire, to keep him at a manageable distance. Easier but infinitely less rewarding. So what if the rewards would not last a lifetime?

She hesitantly lifted the phone off the hook. Jenny's voice was so clear that for a minute Gracie almost believed that she was calling from her upstairs flat.

'Where are you?' she asked, wondering if she would now automatically steel herself against the worst every time the telephone rang. 'I got your note. Have you any idea how worried I've been about you?'

Jenny laughed happily. 'We're in London, Gracie. Buckingham Palace, tea and scones, rain every day!'

'London?' Gracie asked incredulously.

'Don't sound so amazed! Have you forgotten that Rickie is on a course in Europe next week? We decided to detour to London before Paris. We just thought that we'd travel over early so that we could get married. We could have got married somewhere in New York, but London seemed much more romantic, and it's—well, home. I wish you could have been there, Gracie.' There was a hint of sadness in her voice, but not enough to make Gracie believe that that would have made her sister have any second thoughts about her clandestine flight.

'When are you going to be back over here?' she asked.

'When Rickie's course is finished,' Jenny said promptly.

It seemed incredible that, after years of her trying to control her sister, Jenny's life was now totally under control, and in what appeared to be record time. Gracie could feel herself becoming nostalgic and she quickly began to chat, listening to her sister rattle on about their decision, their trip over, the register office wedding, their hotel. Her exuberance spilled down the line and seemed to fill up the whole flat.

'Was Morgan very angry?' Jenny asked. 'Rickie will be on that course after all, so that should please him at any rate, if nothing else does.' She didn't sound as though Morgan's pleasure or displeasure was really of paramount importance, but then Jenny had never been one to brood over other people's opinions of her. She had always done her own thing, either apologetically, or, more often than not, with a total disregard for anyone. It was all part of what Gracie had always seen as her sister's tremendous ingenuousness.

'He *was* angry,' Gracie commented neutrally, 'but he isn't any longer. I think his attitude now is that it's your life, so good luck to you both.'

'What changed him?' Jenny asked with curiosity. 'Rickie was convinced he'd be livid. He said that, once Morgan's made up his mind on something, he never changes it.'

'Which just goes to prove that Rickie was wrong.' At least, she thought, she had managed to help smooth things over between Morgan and his nephew. It would be a small comfort when she faced the long winter nights on her own, but it gave her a good feeling nevertheless.

She replaced the receiver and spent the next fifteen minutes hurriedly getting into her work clothes.

The irony wasn't lost on her that, just as Jenny's chaotic life was running smoothly, her own controlled existence was falling apart.

She arrived at her office on the dot of nine, and immediately felt a fluttering nervousness in the pit of her stomach when she saw Morgan's lean frame by her desk, his fingers swiftly leafing through some papers.

Love, she thought with resigned frustration. Who needed it? Before she had met Morgan, she had never been subjected to this nervous anticipation which made her feel like a teenager on her first date.

The grey eyes flicked over her, lingering on her flushed face and breasts, then he smiled slowly. She wondered how he would treat her now that they were lovers, but when he did speak it was about work, and she realised that he was not going to let any intimacy between them get in the way of their job. She was surprised she had even fleetingly suspected that he might behave otherwise. He was just too much of a professional to let that astute mind of his shake its leash, and catapult itself into areas which would begin to interfere with his concentration.

Gracie buried herself in her work, feeling herself relax as the day wore on, relieved that at least during office hours she could submerge herself in the normality of her everyday routine.

When, just as she was preparing to leave, he asked her, almost casually, whether he could see her that evening, she felt her heart speed up and she accepted, looking away just in case her eyes betrayed too much of what was going on inside her head.

As the days melted into weeks, and the long hot days of summer gradually meandered into golden autumn, it was to become the pattern of their relationship.

At work he was always the cool-headed businessman, creating wealth with that single-minded and intuitive talent which made him so formidable, and she was always his secretary. On only a very few occasions had she looked up suddenly to find the grey eyes fixed on her with what was more than just professional interest, but what exactly they expressed she could never quite define, however hard she tried.

Outside work, when they met, they spent hours passionately locked together. The steel hardness of his eyes would be replaced by a smouldering hunger, which matched her own seemingly inexhaustible hunger for him.

Gracie sometimes felt as though she was in limbo, increasingly aware that their relationship would be her undoing, but too much in love with him to find the courage to step out of it.

It would have been nice to have talked with Jenny about it, but how could she? Discretion was not one of her sister's more outstanding virtues, and besides Jenny was too heavily wrapped up in her own life anyway. She had returned to New York pregnant and happy and full of advice on the joys of married life.

'I never thought I'd see the day when you were the contented housewife,' Gracie had said the last time they had met for lunch, and had grinned when Jenny had responded tartly,

'Please! I intend to regain my figure in record time after the baby's born, and I still dye my hair! I haven't changed that much!'

No, Gracie had thought, all the changing had been done on her side.

Towards the end of October, when the hard cold of winter was already beginning to nudge its way tentatively into Manhattan, Gracie decided, on the spur of the moment, to go to one of the more popular nightclubs with some friends from work. Morgan was entertaining clients, and the thought of a night on her own was not appealing. Solitude no longer held the same attraction for her as it once did. It gave her too much time to think.

Besides, apart from restaurants and theatres, she had seen precious little of New York night life, and this particular club came heavily recommended. It was popular with some of the hierarchy in the company, and she had even heard it mentioned by Morgan who occasionally took foreign clients there as a nightcap after they had been out for dinner. He had once told her that it gave them the illusion of seeing a more decadent side of New York, even though the place was discreetly elegant and very conservative by Manhattan standards.

Gracie's two friends worked together in the accounts department and they shared a small flat in Greenwich Village. They were both similar in temperament, and wildly different from Gracie. They changed boyfriends with a regularity which had become something of a standing joke in their office, and had thankfully abandoned their efforts at trying to introduce Gracie to their small army of cast-off boyfriends, most of whom still appeared to keep in touch with them.

Gracie had just finished changing when they arrived and she looked at them with mock amusement. They were both wearing brightly coloured outfits. She felt like a sparrow in a cage of parrots and she told them so, laughing off their attempts to persuade her into something less elegantly muted.

The nightclub was already very crowded by the time they arrived. It had the statutory dim and semi-lit ambience, but a quick glance showed that the décor was expensive and well chosen, as were most of the people there.

Two bars, one specialising in cocktails only, lined each of the walls and the tables were spread in a semicircle around the dance-floor. A lace-like formation of large potted plants was dotted throughout the room, and Gracie thought that through half-closed eyes you could almost imagine it as somewhere plucked from the roaring nineteen twenties.

The steady beat of the music drummed in the background. Gracie drank two cocktails in quick succession, determined to have no more, and began to relax.

She intended to enjoy herself that evening. Lately she had felt that she was drifting into the dangerous situation of only being able to really have fun when she was in Morgan's company. When he wasn't around, she felt as though a chunk of her was missing, as though she was only half alive.

She chatted animatedly to her friends, laughed a lot and firmly told herself that Morgan Drake was not the be-all and end-all of her existence, and that it was quite possible to be relaxed and carefree without him.

She was almost beginning to believe it when, under the soft gold lighting on the dance-floor, she made out two figures dancing not very far away from where she was sitting. She felt her body stiffen. Everything faded into the background—the music, the tipsy chatter of Jackie and Caroline, the glass of Perrier water which she was holding in her hand, the crowds of people. Everything faded away apart from that couple on the dance-floor. Morgan and Alex.

Alex was wearing a slinky, glittering dress with almost no back at all, and of a soft material that clung to her body like film. Her arms were around Morgan's neck in a stranglehold.

Gracie wanted to tear her eyes away from the interlocked bodies, but for some reason she couldn't. With a masochistic impulse she stared at them in fascination, feeling her heart stop when Morgan's grey eyes met hers with a startled expression.

She looked away abruptly then. Her hand was trembling when she rested her glass gently on the table. Only one thought screamed in her head: the creep, the deceitful, treacherous creep.

He had never proclaimed undying love for her, but she had never expected that he might be seeing other women while he was involved with her, however casual he might consider his involvement. The thought that Alex had been hovering there in the background hit Gracie like a punch in the stomach.

All she wanted to do was to leave. She looked at her friends, her mind searching for some plausible reason she might give them for getting up and walking out, although they had only been there for slightly less than two hours.

'Must go to the Ladies,' she said, hearing the unsteadiness in her voice and feeling it in her legs as she rose from the table.

Painful thoughts and images were racing around in her head, unleashed and frightening in their intensity. It was a physical relief to step into the calm quiet of the plush Ladies and sink heavily on to one of the deep chairs.

She lay back and closed her eyes and allowed herself to succumb to the dizzy, drowning sensation flowing over her.

Wasn't this the awful moment of truth which she had done her best to avoid thinking about for so long? Hadn't she known that she and Morgan were a twosome built on fragility and destined to go nowhere? Well, she thought miserably, this was the inevitable nowhere. This sick, sinking pit that was slowly absorbing her.

She felt a presence, even before she opened her eyes and saw Alex standing in front of her, her thin eyebrows arched in disdain, her eyes hard and glittering.

'I thought I recognised you,' Alex said coolly. Her lips twisted into a mimicry of a smile.

Gracie did not say anything, but she straightened and reached for her bag which she had dumped next to her. The very last thing she needed just now was a slanging match, and from the tight little expression on Alex's face that was precisely what she had in mind.

'Not rushing off, I hope,' Alex remarked, sitting gracefully on the chair closest to Gracie. 'I thought we might have a little chat. It's been quite a while since we saw each other, and there are a few things that I've been meaning to tell you.'

'Oh, really?' Gracie said expressionlessly. Alex had not changed at all in the past months. If anything she seemed even more impeccable than Gracie remembered. She felt a swift stab of jealousy and made an effort to control the trembling in her voice when she next spoke. 'I thought you had already warned me about Morgan, or are you going to be treading old ground?'

'Rumour has it that you two are a going concern.' There was the slightest hint of a question in Alex's voice and Gracie remained silent, wishing she could be any-

where else but where she was. Alex must have seen her
leaving the table and followed her. Was this what a
relationship with Morgan Drake did to a woman? Made
her bitter and resentful months after it had ended, as
Alex so clearly was? Was this how she herself would be
in six months' time? Eight months? Forever?

The prospect engulfed her with dismay and horror.

'You shouldn't listen to rumours,' she replied listlessly.

'Morgan and I may be finished,' Alex continued, her
lips twisting into a hard sneer, 'but that doesn't mean
that you've replaced me as the love of his life. Morgan
knows nothing about love and he doesn't want to. Oh,
yes, he's smooth and charming, he knows how to treat
a woman, but love doesn't enter into the equation.' Her
tone was staccato, hard, like pellets of ice on a tin roof.
'Believe me when I tell you that you're no different from
the rest. Do you really think you have what it takes to
hold him?' Her eyes swept frostily over Gracie, implying
that if *she* didn't have what it took, then no one did,
least of all a secretary of no outstanding physical
attributes.

Every word pierced into Gracie's heart, but she refused
to show what she was feeling. She looked at Alex with
an expression of pity, and derived a twinge of satisfaction
at seeing the anger which it evoked in the other woman.

'Has he ever told you that he loved you?' Alex said,
a fraction more shrilly. She laughed. 'Has he made a
commitment? Ask yourself that, and then ask yourself
why. You're no match for him. He'll take you for as
long as he wants to and then he'll drop you without a
qualm.' She stood up and smoothed her hands over the
contours of her clinging dress. 'But of course, if all these
rumours are simply rumours, then you have nothing to
worry about.' She laughed again and walked away and
Gracie could still hear the laughter ringing in her ears
when she made her way back to the table. The laughter,
and every single word, each of which had been spoken
out of envy and malice but each of which now forced

her to face those questions which she had been struggling to avoid.

I must get out of here, she thought, pain making her frantic. The music had stopped by the time she regained her seat at the table and she was about to make her excuses to her friends, grab her bag and run, when she felt a tap on her shoulder.

She turned round to see Morgan standing behind her, and only just managed to control the temptation to throw the remnants of her Perrier water in his face. Instead she gave him a frozen smile. She could feel her panic and anger throbbing in her veins and she clenched her fists tightly on her lap.

Jackie and Caroline stared at Morgan and then looked nervously at each other. Gracie almost felt sorry for them. Like everyone else in the company they were in awe of him. Now they began chatting uncomfortably, with quick, small smiles, and he made a few innocuous remarks which Gracie didn't take in.

Her mind would not let her take anything in because it was too filled with the lingering image of Alex and Morgan wrapped up with each other, their bodies so entwined that you would have thought they had been glued together. Too filled with the twisted sentiments that had poured from Alex's mouth.

She could feel him inclining slightly over her and every instinct in her screamed to get away from him.

When he leaned forward and said in a flat, even voice that he wanted to dance with her, Gracie had to grit her teeth together to stop herself from being downright rude.

'I was just about to leave, actually,' she said tightly, glaring at Caroline and Jackie when they shot her a surprised look.

'Not until we've danced,' Morgan said in a hard voice.

'Is that a command?' Gracie asked coldly, twisting to face him, and speaking in a voice too low to be heard by her friends.

'Yes.'

'We're not in the office now, you know,' Gracie hissed under her breath. She had risen to her feet and she glared up at him, sweeping her hair away from her face with an impatient movement.

Her body felt ice-cold, and every movement was an effort of will. She wanted to burst into tears and punch him on his chest as hard as she could, hopefully breaking something because that was what he had done to her. He had played with her and now she felt as though she had been dropped, and every bit of her had shattered into a million pieces.

'We're outside work,' she continued in the same glacial voice, 'and what I do outside work is none of your business. I don't want to dance with you, I don't want to talk to you, in fact I damn well don't want to be anywhere near you.'

Out of the corner of her eye she could see Jackie and Caroline talking hesitantly to each other in subdued voices, occasionally throwing her an anxious glance.

Morgan's brows met and his lips compressed into a fine, angry line.

'Speech finished?' he asked tightly, gripping her wrist with his hand and pulling her towards the dance-floor.

'Let me go!' Gracie tugged away, but her action immediately caused his grip to tighten. 'I don't have anything to say to you!' She balked at the thought of making a public scene, even though she could feel her rage bubbling inside her, waiting to explode.

Morgan slipped his arm around her waist, and Gracie stood rigidly against him. 'Listen to me, Gracie,' he snarled, inclining his body so that he was speaking directly into her hair. 'I'm here with clients. I happened to meet Alex purely by accident and she dragged me up to the dance-floor. What the hell did you want me to do?'

'I don't care,' Gracie whispered. 'I don't want to discuss it.' She tried to block out the sharp pain coursing through her, to concentrate on some image that would dull the fierce, nightmarish pounding of her heart, but it was impossible. Every nerve in her body was alive with the thought of Morgan and Alex together, in each other's arms, swaying in time to the music.

'I'm taking you out of here,' Morgan said shortly. 'This is no place to discuss anything.'

'Oh, I'm going all right, but not with you.'

'We'll see about that.' Without giving her time to protest, he pulled her along to the large circular table where four men were seated, one of whom was another director from Morgan's company.

From what seemed like a long way away, she heard him introduce her to them as his secretary, and apologetically tell them that she had taken ill and that he felt it his duty to see her to her flat, and that he would be in touch with them the following Monday to finalise their deal. They all murmured sympathetically, and with uncharacteristic lack of generosity Gracie wondered why, since none of them, apart from the company director, knew her from Eve.

He was right about one thing. She certainly didn't feel well. Her head was spinning and the dark, intimate atmosphere of the club had suddenly become intensely claustrophobic. Had the music been quite so loud as this? Earlier on she had found it pleasantly subdued, but now it was throbbing in her head.

'What about Alex?' Gracie bit out sarcastically. 'Isn't she going to be a little bit disappointed that her Tarzan won't be rounding up the evening in bed with her?'

'Get your bag,' Morgan said between gritted teeth, ignoring her remark, his fingers biting horribly into the fleshy part of her arm. 'And smile when you say goodbye to your pals.'

The smile was more like a weak grimace, and when Jackie asked her if anything was wrong she said weakly that she had a headache.

She didn't care what suspicions her behaviour would give rise to, didn't much care if the entire office, the whole of New York, was buzzing with gossip about her the following Monday when she returned to work. From

what Alex had said, it already was anyway. All she
wanted right now was to get away as fast as her legs
could take her.

Morgan still had his hand on her arm as she wearily
collected her coat in the foyer.

The air was cold when they stepped outside. She felt
it sting her cheeks and whip her hair gently across her
face.

'Now,' he said with ominous calm, 'we're going to
discuss this in private. My car's parked across the road.'
His hand didn't slacken as he opened the passenger door
of the car and waited until she had sat down.

'Where are we going?' Gracie asked dully. As soon as
the words were out she realised that it was a stupid
question, because she knew that they were going to her
flat. She recognised the neon signs as the car purred
towards the Lincoln Center.

Morgan had not answered her. In fact, he did not
speak for the short duration of the journey, and the grim
tightness did not leave his lips. When the car pulled up
in front of the apartment block, he switched off the
ignition and turned towards her.

'So you saw me with Alex,' he said shortly, 'and with
an extraordinary leap of logic you've decided that two
and two must make four.'

'You're wrong. I know you're finished with her.' I
heard it from the horse's mouth, she thought bitterly.
Oh, no, that's not what's bothering me. What's giving
me this sick, churning feeling is what Alex said, is having
all my doubts confirmed by her.

'Well, what, then?'

He stared at her with a puzzled expression. Obviously
he had not seen Alex follow her into the Ladies, and
Gracie had no intention of enlightening him as to the
content of their conversation, if conversation was what
it could be called.

'I just felt a little sick, that's all. I must have drunk
more than I thought. I just want to get to bed. By myself.
Without the pleasure of your company.' She turned the

door-handle, steeling herself to walk away from him without exposing what she was feeling.

'Not so fast, Gracie.'

There was a threatening note to his voice, but that didn't bother her one bit. He had hurt her and there was nothing more he could do that could make her feel any worse. Of course, she thought bitterly, she had deferred the inevitable until the inevitable decided to make the first move. So she only had herself to blame. Still, that did not lessen her anger.

'Well if you have anything else to say, then hurry up. I just want to go upstairs and be by myself.' Her tone conveyed long-suffering patience, as though any second now she would look at her watch and yawn. She could tell that he didn't like it. His eyes narrowed and he looked furious enough to throttle her.

'Just who do you think you are?' he muttered brusquely. 'Do you think that because we're sleeping together you have a right to play the heavy-handed mistress with me?'

'I have never done anything of the sort!'

His accusation hurt because she had made it a point never to be possessive with him. She had accepted their relationship on his terms because she was in love with him.

He'll never make a commitment to you, she remembered Alex saying. She was right. Wasn't this his implication now?

'What are you doing now?'

Gracie laughed cynically. 'No one means anything to you, do they?' she found herself asking, driven to hear it once and for all from his own lips. 'Unless you're leading the relationship, taking what you want out of it, you don't give a damn about anything else!'

'Listen to yourself for a minute!' Morgan's voice was getting more angry. 'You act as though you're my wife! I'm sorry to disappoint you, but you're not my wife, and you have no claim on me whatsoever.'

'I realise that,' Gracie bit out, hearing her voice as though from miles away, carried away on a tide of aching fury that made her want to lash out at him. 'Has anyone ever had any claim on you? Will anyone ever?'

'No!'

They stared at each other in the semi-darkness of the car. The grey of his eyes were like pieces of flint.

'Commitment isn't part of what I have to offer,' he said roughly, 'I saw my father destroyed by love. Oh, everything was rosy, for a while. Isn't that always the way? But then my mother grew bored with him, bored with his work. I've seen what love can do. By the time she walked out on him he was a shell, broken. Well, I've learnt from that.'

So this was it, Gracie thought, her insides twisting with a depth of misery which surpassed everything she had ever imagined she could feel. He had made his position perfectly clear—she meant nothing to him other than an enjoyable sexual object. To have him say it was like hearing a painful truth shouted out from the rooftops.

'I see,' Gracie whispered. It was all she could find to say. The feelings rushing through her could find no words. So Alex was right. Not just Alex. She herself had been right all along. She had lived in a bubble of pretence, hoping against reason that he would somehow grow to love her the way that she loved him. She had been a fool, but it wasn't too late to stop being one.

'You accepted me for what I was,' he said grimly, his strong hands clenched tightly on the steering-wheel of the car. 'I never promised anything I couldn't deliver.'

'No,' Gracie muttered coldly, feeling the sting of tears behind her eyelids.

'Well, did you think that you were different from the rest? Did you?' Morgan looked at her savagely. Did he really expect her to answer that question? Could she? 'I never forced you into anything. It was up to you to choose what you wanted, and you did.'

'It's also up to me to choose not to continue working for you,' Gracie said with cold precision. 'As of this moment I resign, so you can go and find yourself another secretary and another bed partner.'

The words were uttered before she could swallow them down and Morgan greeted her statement with silence. He turned away abruptly and stared through the window.

'If that's what you want,' he muttered, 'then go ahead and resign. You'll never find a better job.'

'Don't bet on it!' She would never admit it, not in a million years, but he was right. Morgan had encouraged her to attain a degree of responsibility in her work which she would find nowhere else.

'You and your talk of commitment,' he said thickly. 'You women are all the same. I was a fool, I thought you were different. You and I seemed to be on the same wavelength.'

Sorry to have disappointed you, Gracie thought acidly.

'Goodbye, Morgan.' She opened the car door and stepped outside, catching her breath at the sudden blanket of cold.

She began walking towards the block of apartments, her jaw clenched so hard to stop the tears from spilling over that her face ached. She heard Morgan snap open his door and she hurried.

'Damn you, Gracie!' he bellowed. 'You can damn well leave for all I care! I don't need you!'

She heard the car door slam and then the furious revving of the car as it swung around and was lost in the network of streets.

There was a dead, hollow feeling in her when she let herself into her apartment. She didn't even bother to switch on the lights, stumbling through the darkness until she made her way to her bedroom, then she sat on the bed and allowed herself the luxury of crying. Quiet tears at first, then deep, racking sobs that left her feeling drained and weary.

She had seen it coming, she thought miserably, hadn't she? She had known all along what sort of man Morgan was. She could have written a book on the senselessness of becoming involved with him, but even so, she had been drawn irresistibly into his web, and when she could have taken the opportunity of turning away she had chosen to become his lover. Face it, she thought as she brushed her teeth and stared at her puffy reflection in the mirror, you behaved like a lovesick teenager unable to run away from the power of your emotions.

She knew that her spontaneous decision to leave her job was the only thing she could do now. She would phone in ill on the Monday, and take the opportunity to book an immediate flight back to London.

The thought of never seeing Morgan again, never catching that lazy heaviness in his eyes when they made love, never hearing the deep timbre of his voice, was unbearable.

She slept restlessly, haunted by vivid, frustrated dreams that left her feeling as though she had not slept at all when she awakened the following morning.

The first thing she did was to pack her belongings, tossing them randomly into her suitcases which she had never got around to changing, and which were even more precarious-looking than she remembered.

It didn't take long. She had indulged in some clothes-buying over the past few months, but had not purchased anything bulky. She was grateful now that she had not, because there would literally have been no room in her cases in which to pack anything else.

She knew that she would have to tell Jenny of her plans, and she did so with a heavy heart.

'But you can't go, Gracie!' she wailed down the line. 'I want you to be with me when the baby's born!'

Gracie winced. She had been looking forward to the event almost as much as her sister had been, and it hurt to know that she would not be able to share those first moments with her niece.

'I'll visit,' she said shakily. When I can think of Morgan rationally, she added silently to herself. 'London isn't the back of beyond, you know!'

By the time she gently replaced the receiver, she felt as though the final step had been taken. There could be no backing out now, even if she had wanted to.

She had revealed only the bare bones of her reasons for leaving New York so abruptly, as much to spare her sister any unnecessary distress as to protect herself. She didn't know a great deal about medicine, but she did know that it was better to spare a pregnant woman any emotional trauma. Besides, she could always write and tell her the full story, when some of the sharpness of the pain had worn off.

The rest of the day seemed to pass by in blurry slow motion. There was an unreality about everything. It puzzled her. She was saying goodbye to the only man she would ever love, and all she felt was this peculiar numbness.

The following morning she phoned the company and spoke to one of the other secretaries who told her that Morgan was in a breakfast meeting.

'Could you tell him that I won't be in today? I've got some kind of stomach bug.' On the spur of the moment she added, 'And if I'm not in tomorrow, then it's for the same reason, but I'll definitely be in on Wednesday.'

'Sure.' She could hear munching noises over the phone, and wondered what Katje was eating. Katje always seemed to be eating, even though she was enviably slim. The thought of food was enough to make Gracie feel quite ill. What a stereotype reaction, she thought cynically, hanging up the phone. Can't eat, can't sleep, what next? And all over a man who probably didn't give her a moment's thought in his spare time.

She took a taxi to JFK Airport, and managed to get a much earlier flight than she had expected. There had apparently been a last-minute cancellation and Gracie took the seat, even though the airline was one of the more expensive ones. She felt almost furtive as she boarded the plane less than two hours later.

Heaven only knows why, she thought. Had she expected to look around and see Morgan rushing through the terminal with flowers in his hand and words of everlasting love on his lips? That was the stuff that soppy advertisements were made of, the stuff of silly daydreams.

It was not until the plane was in the air that she relaxed. An overweight businessman in the seat next to her did his best to initiate a conversation, and Gracie answered his questions with such a lack of enthusiasm that he finally turned his attention to his newspaper, leaving her time to think about everything. Unwelcome thoughts, but ones that would not go away.

She told herself that it would all run its course, and that in time she would put that sliver of life behind her and move on. She wasn't the first person to have suffered from a broken heart. It was hardly a terminal condition.

By the time the in-flight film was ready to begin, Gracie was feeling almost dizzy from a combination of lack of sleep and the onslaught of her emotions.

She drifted into an uncomfortable sleep, and did not awaken until the pilot announced that they were approaching Heathrow.

CHAPTER TEN

LONDON did not seem to have changed at all. Even the skies still held that opaque grey colour which most tourists accepted as part and parcel of British weather. She had left behind grey skies when she had boarded the plane for New York, and now she had returned to them. She might almost be tempted to believe that the intervening months had been no more than a dream, except that the speechless pain in her heart was just too sharp to ignore.

London might have remained the same, but Gracie felt as though she was returning to it years older. She had gone to New York a composed, if somewhat cool young woman. All the compartments in her life had been neatly sealed and categorised, and there had been no room for the unexpected. There was no resemblance between that past and this disordered present.

She had had the foresight to phone her estate agents before leaving America to warn them that she would be returning to her flat at very short notice, and to find alternative arrangements for her lodgers. The woman she had spoken to had been anything but impressed, but in the end she had been forced to accept the situation. Maybe something in Gracie's tone of voice had implied that, however regrettable the circumstance was, there would be no alternative.

As the black cab pulled up outside the building Gracie felt a twinge of anxiety that she would walk into a roomful of strangers because she had not given her tenants sufficient time to vacate the premises, but the place was empty when she opened the front door.

She unburdened herself of her various bags and suit-cases, and went across to the window and stared sight-lessly outside, at a loss what to do next.

There was a dead, heavy feeling inside her. She knew that she should start making plans, not least registering for work, but whenever her brain clicked into gear it began rolling along uncomfortable tracks, began throwing out disturbing and disjointed visions of Morgan, things that she did not want to think about.

Where was logic when you most needed it? Gracie wondered. Nowhere useful, that was for sure. And she didn't feel as if she had the energy to pursue it. She sat down heavily on the sofa and closed her eyes.

She allowed the memories of Morgan to fill every inch of her, not bothering to fight them off, until she felt as though she was being consumed by all those graphic, painful images of him. She tried to imagine how he would have reacted to her departure. He would have been stunned, she knew, but perhaps also a little bit relieved. After all, hadn't she more or less confronted him with her need for his commitment, and wasn't that the last thing in the world that he was looking for? The one thing that guaranteed the early death of any relationship with him?

At least by leaving she was sparing them both the inevitable and distasteful showdown.

She drifted into an uneasy sleep, part of her aware that sleeping was the last thing she ought to be doing when there were cases to unpack and a flat to rearrange. More than a flat, a life to rearrange, for heaven's sake!

The estate agent had thought to leave the central heating switched on, and the place was warm. Not the same as the flat in New York, though, Gracie thought sluggishly; not nearly the same.

The following morning she awoke in her bed, and vaguely remembered having dragged herself into the bedroom and under the duvet, not taking the trouble of removing her clothes.

She also vaguely remembered an inkling of an idea which she had either dreamt or else had managed to slip its way through her muddled thoughts before she had fallen asleep.

She reached for the telephone before she could reason herself out of it, and dialled the number for Collins and Collins, her old firm. After all, hadn't Mr Collins told her to get in touch with him if ever she needed a job? Well, now was a good time to find out whether he was serious or not about his offer.

Everything hurtles back to square one, she thought, as she heard the distinctive tones of her ex-boss.

'My dear!' he exclaimed, surprising her when he recognised her voice immediately. 'I had no idea you had returned to England! Are you over here on holiday?'

Only if by that you mean a permanent vacation, Gracie thought grimly. 'No,' she replied, hoping that he would deduce the reason for her phone call. 'Here to stay.'

'Couldn't take the fast pace of New York, eh?' She heard him chuckle down the line.

'Something like that,' she said, with an attempt to sound light-hearted. She thought of Morgan's dark, handsome face and continued hurriedly, 'I'm phoning, actually, to find out whether there are any vacancies with you for a secretary. I thought that I'd give you a call before I got in touch with the employment agencies, just in case.'

'Well...'

'It's no bother if there aren't,' Gracie interjected quickly. She meant it too. Nice though it might be to slip into a job where she was already familiar with both the people and the work, perhaps it would be too much like a step backwards.

There was no point in trying to turn the clock back. She almost wished she had never contacted her old firm.

'I think we can find something for you,' Mr Collins said thoughtfully. 'We've taken on two new partners since you left and the workload has increased dramatically. The girl I've got working for me would appreciate someone to help her out, and it would be an added bonus that you already know our system here.'

'If you're sure,' Gracie said.

'When would you be able to start?'

'Today?' she replied, glancing at the clock by her bed. It was only nine-fifteen. She would still be able to put in more or less a full day's work, and it would do her good to get out of the flat, to find something to occupy her mind.

'Sure you're not too tired?' Mr Collins sounded puzzled, as though he couldn't quite understand the immediacy of her tone. 'Jet lag and all that sort of thing.'

'Not at all. If it's the same to you, I'd quite like to start immediately.' She tried to camouflage the urgency in her voice by throwing in conversationally, 'There really isn't a great deal to do with the flat and I can unpack and buy some provisions when I get back this evening...'

So at least that sorted a part of her life out, even if only temporarily. She was doing something. Time and the process of healing would have to do the rest.

Very little had changed at her old place of work. She had to keep reminding herself that she had only been away a few months, even though it felt like much longer, like decades. She didn't know whether the familiarity was comforting or unnerving but at least it distracted her from her own problems.

Her colleagues quizzed her about New York, and Gracie told them everything they wanted to know, making sure to leave out any personal details. By lunchtime their curiosity had abated, and by the time six o'clock had rolled round she was beginning to feel as though she had never left the place.

Despite the fact that there were now two new partners, there still wasn't a great deal to be done, and before she left Gracie had a quick chat with Mr Collins to tell him that she would probably be there only temporarily. He nodded his agreement, unconsciously hitting upon the truth when he laughingly asked whether New York had spoilt her by handing her a job with which they could never compete.

'Something like that,' Gracie said with a wry smile. She thought of Morgan striding through his office, tossing ideas at her so quickly that she could barely catch them, his sharp mind always two steps ahead of everyone else's. The smile threatened to waver. 'It was kind of you to take me on when you had no need,' she remarked.

'Oh there's always a need for someone like you around here,' Mr Collins replied. He took off his glasses and carefully cleaned first one lens, then the other, with a piece of tissue. 'I don't know why you returned to England so quickly, Grace, but I could tell from your tone of voice on the phone that you wanted to start back working immediately for more reasons than simply the money. I'm quite happy for you to remain here until you feel strong enough to leave, be that for a week, a month or a year.'

He turned his kindly eyes on her and Gracie felt like bursting into tears. For the second time that day Mr Collins had surprised her. She had always liked him, but they had rarely discussed anything personal. She would certainly never have imagined him to be as astute as he now revealed.

Had she always misjudged everyone? she thought to herself. The only person she seemed able to read accurately was herself. She had admitted her love for Morgan from the very beginning, but from that she had derived only a dubious satisfaction tempered with more pain than she cared to think about.

By the time she left the building darkness had already settled like a shroud.

It seemed darker over here than it did in New York. Perhaps that was because there were fewer lights and far fewer people. Out of habit she hailed a taxi and allowed herself the luxury of being driven back to her flat. With no generous boss to cover such expenses, it was an extravagance which she would have to do away with soon enough, but she was in no mood to battle her way through the Underground system. That little reality, she thought, would have to be postponed at least until the next day. There was little chance of finding a job in London that paid anything near what she had been getting in New York. She would have to begin pulling in her belt, making economies and generally avoiding such things as unnecessary taxi trips.

It was just as well that she had managed to save some of her salary before returning to London. It would stand her in good stead.

The thought immediately conjured up the dauntingly lonely picture of long empty evenings stretching into infinity.

Gracie grimaced and squeezed her eyes shut. She told herself that everything had a beginning, a middle and an end. Why, she thought miserably, did her beginning and middle have to be so short and the ending so long? A lifetime, in fact?

She was almost unaware of the taxi's pulling up outside her flat. She hurriedly paid the driver and walked up to the door, fumbling in her bag for her key-ring.

With an instinctive movement she turned the doorknob before inserting the key and felt the door click open. Gracie started back in surprise. She was sure she had locked up before she had left for work that morning. Positive. It would have been inconceivable leaving the house open.

Burglars, she thought. Maybe she should call the police. She looked around and saw that the taxi was no longer in sight. Her hand was perspiring as she cautiously pushed open the door, ready to turn tail and run if there was even the slightest suspicion that there was anyone inside.

She took little steps inside, edging towards the light switch. There was a rustling sound and she swung round, her eyes widening in fright as she took in the figure seated on the sofa. With jangling nerves she slammed her hand on the light switch and the darkness became Technicolor.

Gracie stared at Morgan, who had not risen from the sofa, unable to control the shock and disbelief that coloured her face. She was still clutching her bag tightly and her heart seemed to have stopped beating, frozen into a state of numbness, which was how the rest of her felt.

'Surprised to see me?' he asked with overwhelming understatement.

The grey eyes were fixed on her. He seemed to be totally in control. There he was, sitting in the lounge of *her* flat, having given her the fright of her life merely by *being* there, and displaying all the calm of someone not in the slightest bit perturbed.

'What are you doing here? And how on earth did you get in?'

'One question at a time,' he told her, 'and not until you've sat down. You look as though you'd just seen a ghost.'

'What do you expect?' Gracie's voice rose. 'I didn't exactly think that I'd walk into my flat to find you sitting in it!'

The worst part was that she could feel her body trembling with pleasure at the sight of him. She wanted to feast her eyes on him, because she knew that, if he had followed her to England so that he could try and persuade her to prolong their affair, then she would have no alternative but to refuse.

'Why did you run away?' he asked bluntly.

'You haven't answered either of my questions,' Gracie prevaricated. She self-consciously removed her coat, knowing that it was idiotic to be embarrassed as his eyes swept possessively over her. After all, hadn't they lain naked in each other's arms? Countless times? Nevertheless she shifted her gaze away from his face as she sank on to one of the chairs, tucking her feet underneath her.

'I can't discuss my reasons for coming here when you're sitting so far away from me. I feel as if I'm being interviewed.'

Gracie knew what he meant. There was something oddly painful about being so physically close to him, yet unable to reach out and touch him. Would it hurt to at least sit next to him? she thought. They were both adults. Why act like children? It was hardly as though he was going to rape her!

She hesitantly stepped towards the sofa, watching as his eyes darkened until they were a smouldering, charcoal colour. She could feel a sense of yearning flood through her body, filling every inch of her, making the hairs on her arms seem to stand on end.

She sat next to him, her thigh lightly brushing his. She half expected him to put his arm around her, and was almost disappointed when he left them folded across his chest.

'Isn't that better?' he asked in a low, soft voice.

'Are you going to tell me why you've come here?' She could not look at him, so she stared fixedly at her slim fingers.

'Persistent little creature, aren't you? I should have recognised that from the very first moment I laid eyes on you. Maybe it would have warned me off.' He leaned to face her, and her body shuddered as he stroked her arm with his finger. It was a gesture that was more tender and thoughtful than erotic, but it still made her breathing quicken as she responded involuntarily to his touch.

'I didn't want to follow you to England,' Morgan intoned in a low voice. He might almost have been talking to himself. 'I knew that, if I did, it would be an acknowledgement of the fact that my solid, reliable bachelor life was well and truly over.'

Gracie felt her heart leap with a sweet ache and she controlled the desire to blurt out her love for him, to wrap her arms around his neck. After all, wasn't it possible that this was all part of a ploy to try and persuade her to continue being his mistress? She knew that she was being uncharitable, but to allow herself to melt, even the tiniest bit, was to court danger. Hadn't she been provided with ample proof of what this man could do to her?

'I never gave you an ultimatum,' she said truthfully.

'You left, ran away. Don't you think that that was far worse than any ultimatum you could ever have given me?'

'I didn't want to put you in an invidious position.' Gracie chose her words carefully, wanting to be honest rather than defensive. She looked at him warily from under her lashes, trying to read the expression on his face. 'You as much as told me that you weren't interested in relationships, except for the sexual ones, that is, and I knew that you weren't lying. I would have hated myself if I had tried to force you out of your freedom.'

Their eyes met and he muttered, 'Oh, Gracie,' then he lowered his mouth to hers, his lips moving fiercely over hers.

Gracie returned his kiss, abandoning any attempt at resistance. His tongue probed her mouth; she tasted its sweetness and felt her limbs grow heavy and feverish with desire.

When he got to his feet, lifting her in his arms, she allowed her head to fall against his chest, unprotesting as he carried her to the bedroom, kicking shut the door behind him.

It took a minute or so for her eyes to adjust to the darkness in the room. Morgan was standing next to the bed, looking down at her, his fingers slowly unbuttoning his shirt.

'You can relieve me of the rest,' he murmured, slipping underneath the covers with her. He had loved her to undress him, and she did so now, slowly, dizzy anticipation filling her as much as she knew it was filling him. It felt like years since she had touched his body!

She unfastened the clasp of his trousers and he shrugged them off. When her fingers slipped underneath the band of his underwear, he groaned huskily, and his body trembled as she caressed him. With jerky movements he stripped her of her clothing, pulling her close to him, so close that Gracie almost had the sensation of being absorbed into him.

'I've been out of my mind with wanting you,' he whispered huskily into her ear. 'When I realised that you had walked out on me, I felt a thousand different things, anger, pain, bewilderment at the power that you had over me; most of all I wanted to find you, to touch you, to feel your beautiful, warm body close to mine.'

He swept back her hair so that he could tease her earlobe with his teeth, then his lips were trailing warm, urgent kisses on her neck.

Gracie arched back, breathing quickly, her body quivering for fulfillment and at the same time wanting to prolong the ecstasy she was feeling for as long as possible. His strong hands cupped her breasts and he lightly rolled the hardened nipples between thumb and forefinger.

'Gracie, darling,' he murmured shakily, 'you're my addiction. The more I'm with you, the more I want to be with you, and the more I make love to you, the more I want to continue. Does that make any sense?'

Gracie nodded languorously. It all made perfect sense, because it was precisely how she felt about him.

He stroked apart her thighs with his hand and she closed her eyes as he slid into her, his movements urgent and rhythmic. Their lovemaking was passionate, as if they had not touched each other in years, when in fact it had only been a matter of days.

'Oh, my darling,' he moaned against her neck, 'how could you leave me?'

He shifted his weight alongside her and stroked the hair away from her face with tender, careful fingers, as though she were made of china.

'Was it because you saw me with Alex at that club? I swear to you that it was pure coincidence. I said goodbye to her a long time ago, and believe me I had not the slightest intention of renewing my acquaintanceship with her. And never will. You must believe me.'

Gracie believed him, and she told him so. 'Seeing you with Alex only served to make me decide on something which was inevitable,' she said awkwardly. She nervously traced a pattern on his chest and he caught her finger, nipping it gently between his teeth.

'Meaning?'

Morgan stared at her fixedly. Isn't it obvious? Gracie thought, lowering her eyes. She felt as transparent as if she had been made of glass, as if the workings of her mind were on display for him to read. She was sure he was aware of exactly what she was trying to say to him, but wanted her to admit it aloud instead of verbally beating about the bush. This was the confrontation she had dreaded. Suddenly she no longer did. She loved him. Why bother to hide it?

'Meaning . . .' Gracie nevertheless ventured hesitantly, 'that I know what you want out of a relationship, and it's not what I want. I became your lover because I wanted to and because in a sense I almost couldn't help myself. I thought that I could love you and ask nothing in return, but I was wrong. So I did the cowardly thing, and I ran away.'

Morgan drew a sharp breath. 'You love me,' he stated, as though liking the sound of the expression. 'You love me.'

Gracie trembled, reaching to loop her arms around his neck.

'I felt your love,' he continued. 'I just didn't realise how much I needed it until I woke up to find you gone. Do you know that I wanted you from the very first instant I saw you? You walked into my office with that cool, brave expression on your face, all ready to start a fight on behalf of your sister, and I took one look at you and had to fight against the attraction.'

Gracie smiled and curled her body against his. The word 'permanency' had not entered their conversation, but she liked what he was telling her, felt each word warming her, enveloping her in its perfect folds.

'Why didn't you tell me any of this before?' she asked softly, returning the tiny kisses that he was placing on her lips.

'Because, well...I don't really know.'

His face reddened suddenly and she wanted to giggle. There was something unbearably vulnerable about his expression. She thought that he would be even more red-faced if he could see himself in a mirror.

'You don't know?' she asked with mock incredulity. 'And here I was, thinking that you knew everything.'

Morgan chuckled.

'You've always made it your habit to drag everything out of me, and now I want you to tell me what you're thinking,' she said.

'I'm thinking that I was a fool.' His fingers brushed the underside of her breast and Gracie shuddered. 'I tried to kid myself that what I felt for you was attraction and nothing more, perhaps some fondness. You see, I could handle a relationship based on sex, but anything else...well...I had no experience, never thought there was a place for that in my life. So when you appeared on the scene and proceeded to turn my world upside-down I was afraid and a little confused. I had convinced myself from an early age that what happened to my father would never happen to me.'

She remembered what he had told her about his parents and understood that he had locked himself into a prison of invulnerability the same way she had. They had both thought love was controllable, like a job, or a hobby.

His hands were caressing her intimately and she could feel a drowsy passion filling her.

'Do you think that it was any easier for me to admit that I had fallen head over heels in love with you?' Gracie asked. 'Believe me, my safe little world was taking a beating as well.'

'Good,' Morgan teased.

'I could tell from the beginning that you spelt trouble, and, as if my own intuitions weren't enough, Alex did a fine job of warning me off you when we met at that little house party of yours.' Not to mention later, she thought without resentment.

'The bitch!' He looked at her, his face grim. 'I suspected she had done something of the sort. She began making snide comments about you and I saw red. I dragged her off to the privacy of the poolside and gave her a piece of my mind.'

Gracie remembered. She had seen them in the semidarkness, standing by the pool, and had immediately assumed that they were escaping from the crowds inside to the privacy outside. She vaguely remembered thinking at the time that if they could not keep their hands off each other in company, then lord knew what they got up to once they were on their own.

'And to make matters worse,' he carried on, 'I returned to the house in a foul temper, only to be confronted with you flirting outrageously with that child.'

'Child?'

'Anthony Palmer. I'd never had murderous urges before, but I looked at the two of you and felt that I could have quite easily thrown him in a cell and chucked away the key.'

Gracie laughed out loud at that and began explaining her friendship with Tony, but she was silenced by Morgan's mouth, pressing fiercely on hers. She melted into his kiss, coiling her fingers into his dark hair as he bent his head and began sucking on her erect nipples.

When he raised his eyes to hers, her face was flushed.

'I've come to take you back with me, Gracie,' he said quietly, as though she had asked him.

Gracie sighed, squeezing her eyes shut. She wanted to block out the temptation to nod her assent and forget all the reasons that she had left New York in the first place. She loved him, and he might want her desperately, but beyond his longing was a future, her future. She could already foresee the day that he would weary of her, and the thought was enough to make her heart clench in pain.

'I love you, Morgan,' she began hesitantly.

'But you won't be my mistress,' he continued, smiling. Gracie's eyes flew open and she gravely contemplated his face, the perfect set of his features, the firm mouth. 'Have I asked you to be my mistress?' The smile turned to a wry grin. 'I know I haven't exactly been the epitome of stability as far as women are concerned, but you've managed to change all that. I've never been in love before, but I'm in love now, and I can't imagine anything more satisfying than to spend the rest of my life with you.'

'Are you proposing to me?' Gracie asked incredulously.

'Only if you're accepting.'

'I'm accepting.'

She could feel her body relax.

'You don't take much persuading, woman,' Morgan teased, running his hands along her thighs. 'Is this an indication of a lifetime of subservience in store for me?'

'Over my dead body!' They looked at each other and laughed. My heart is about to burst with happiness, Gracie thought. She had a fleeting but vivid image of all the beautiful women that had passed in and out of his life, and said, 'There's something else. No Alexes ever again, and if you happen to run into her, or into anyone else for that matter, then you'd better be prepared to run away in the opposite direction as fast as your legs can take you.'

Morgan's eyes flared. 'Jealous?'

'Definitely.'

'Good. And I hope you see that as conclusive proof of what a poor, trapped man I've become. I actually want you to be possessive with me! Needless to say, the same applies to you.'

Gracie didn't answer. She smiled, running her fingers along his lean body.

'Jenny will be more than a little surprised by these developments,' she said absent-mindedly.

'I doubt it.'

'You do?'

Morgan nodded. 'Who do you think gave me the key to get into your flat? I told her that the next time she saw you you would be married, to me.'

'Sure of yourself, weren't you?' Gracie teased, placing a kiss on the corner of his mouth.

'Yes.' Morgan's fingers tangled in her hair as he drew her towards him, his lips parting hers, his tongue exploring her mouth.

'Just imagine, Gracie darling, we'll be able to make love every minute of every day that we spend together, for the rest of our lives.'

Gracie moaned softly in response as his hand travelled the length of her torso to stroke the sweet moistness between her thighs.

His body trembled with desire as she shifted restlessly against his hand.

'I can't wait,' she murmured, and she smiled as her thoughts flew through the window and unseeing, un-reasoning passion took their place.

HARLEQUIN
Romance®

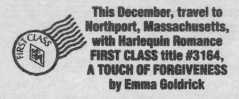

This December, travel to Northport, Massachusetts, with Harlequin Romance FIRST CLASS title #3164, A TOUCH OF FORGIVENESS by Emma Goldrick

Folks in Northport called Kitty the meanest woman in town, but she couldn't forget how they had duped her brother and exploited her family's land. It was hard to be mean, though, when Joel Carmody was around—his calm, good humor made Kitty feel like a new woman. Nevertheless, a Carmody was a Carmody, and the name meant money and power to the townspeople.... Could Kitty really trust Joel, or was he like all the rest?

"INDULGE A LITTLE" SWEEPSTAKES

HERE'S HOW THE SWEEPSTAKES WORKS

NO PURCHASE NECESSARY

To enter each drawing, complete the appropriate Official Entry Form or a 3" by 5" index card by hand-printing your name, address and phone number and the trip destination that the entry is being submitted for (i.e., Walt Disney World Vacation Drawing, etc.) and mailing it to: Indulge '91 Subscribers-Only Sweepstakes, P.O. Box 1397, Buffalo, New York 14269-1397.

No responsibility is assumed for lost, late or misdirected mail. Entries must be sent separately with first class postage affixed, and be received by: 9/30/91 for the Walt Disney World Vacation Drawing, 10/31/91 for the Alaskan Cruise Drawing and 11/30/91 for the Hawaiian Vacation Drawing. Sweepstakes is open to residents of the U.S. and Canada, 21 years of age or older as of 11/7/91.

For complete rules, send a self-addressed, stamped (WA residents need not affix return postage) envelope to: Indulge '91 Subscribers-Only Sweepstakes Rules, P.O. Box 4005, Blair, NE 68009.

DIR-RL

"INDULGE A LITTLE" SWEEPSTAKES

HERE'S HOW THE SWEEPSTAKES WORKS

NO PURCHASE NECESSARY

To enter each drawing, complete the appropriate Official Entry Form or a 3" by 5" index card by hand-printing your name, address and phone number and the trip destination that the entry is being submitted for (i.e., Walt Disney World Vacation Drawing, etc.) and mailing it to: Indulge '91 Subscribers-Only Sweepstakes, P.O. Box 1397, Buffalo, New York 14269-1397.

No responsibility is assumed for lost, late or misdirected mail. Entries must be sent separately with first class postage affixed, and be received by: 9/30/91 for the Walt Disney World Vacation Drawing, 10/31/91 for the Alaskan Cruise Drawing and 11/30/91 for the Hawaiian Vacation Drawing. Sweepstakes is open to residents of the U.S. and Canada, 21 years of age or older as of 11/7/91.

For complete rules, send a self-addressed, stamped (WA residents need not affix return postage) envelope to: Indulge '91 Subscribers-Only Sweepstakes Rules, P.O. Box 4005, Blair, NE 68009.

© 1991 HARLEQUIN ENTERPRISES LTD.   DIR-RL

INDULGE A LITTLE—WIN A LOT!

Summer of '91 Subscribers-Only Sweepstakes

OFFICIAL ENTRY FORM

This entry must be received by: Oct. 31, 1991
This month's winner will be notified by: Nov. 7, 1991
Trip must be taken between: May 27, 1992—Sept. 9, 1992
(depending on sailing schedule)

YES, I want to win the Alaska Cruise vacation for two. I understand the prize includes round-trip airfare, one-week cruise including private cabin, all meals and pocket money as revealed on the "wallet" scratch-off card.

Name _____

Address _____ Apt. _____

City _____

State/Prov. _____ Zip/Postal Code _____

Daytime phone number _____
(Area Code)

Return entries with invoice in envelope provided. Each book in this shipment has two entry coupons—and the more coupons you enter, the better your chances of winning!

© 1991 HARLEQUIN ENTERPRISES LTD.   2N-CPS

INDULGE A LITTLE—WIN A LOT!

Summer of '91 Subscribers-Only Sweepstakes

OFFICIAL ENTRY FORM

This entry must be received by: Oct. 31, 1991
This month's winner will be notified by: Nov. 7, 1991
Trip must be taken between: May 27, 1992—Sept. 9, 1992
(depending on sailing schedule)

YES, I want to win the Alaska Cruise vacation for two. I understand the prize includes round-trip airfare, one-week cruise including private cabin, all meals and pocket money as revealed on the "wallet" scratch-off card.

Name _____

Address _____ Apt. _____

City _____

State/Prov. _____ Zip/Postal Code _____

Daytime phone number _____
(Area Code)

Return entries with invoice in envelope provided. Each book in this shipment has two entry coupons—and the more coupons you enter, the better your chances of winning!

© 1991 HARLEQUIN ENTERPRISES LTD.   2N-CPS